A
SECOND
HAND
LIE

Thank you for your support,
and I hope you enjoy the book.
Hugs!

Pamela Crane

A
SECOND
HAND
LIE

A Short Thriller

PAMELA CRANE

Tabella House
Raleigh, North Carolina

Thank you for supporting authors and literacy by purchasing this book. Want to add more gripping reads to your library? As the author of more than a dozen award-winning and best-selling books, you can find all of Pamela Crane's works on her website at www.pamelacrane.com.

To my family.

Although it isn't perfect, it's mine.

History is a set of lies agreed upon.
– Napoléon Bonaparte

Man is not what he thinks he is. He is what he hides.
– André Malraux

Prologue

1992

On the day that Ruby Parker was shot, someone got away with murder. Not the pop-culture type of murder that the media fixates on with macabre fascination as gory details permeate the news, but the loss of a life, nonetheless. A loss that would cause a domino effect of misery in an endless wake of suffering. A loss that would galvanize a heart to stop feeling, cementing the true victim's emotions in a state of perpetual sadness.

That victim was me, Landon Worthington, and this is my story of loss and redemption.

At age sixteen I'm already a byproduct of bad luck—a couple of battered souls that never should have hooked up to produce spawn. Alcoholic parents who never understood the value of the dollar wasted on... well, getting wasted. A ramshackle house in a neighborhood that bred poverty. A sister dragged into a serial killer's twisted desire to "help" her, which took her life far too soon.

Maybe it was tragedy. Or maybe she escaped. I wasn't sure which.

I'll never erase my first memory. Age three. I had grabbed the carton of milk from the fridge, wrestling the too-heavy container to the floor where I proceeded to feebly drain it into an unwashed cup I had found on the table. My weak arms couldn't sustain it, and as expected, the milk ended up in a puddle at my feet. Normal childhood mistake, right? Not to my father. Based on the beating I got, you would've thought I'd totaled the car. The wounds from my whipping bled

1

through the seat of my pants for days. After that, I learned how to retreat. I've been doing it ever since.

In the pregnant pause between my birth and death, life had become little more than a series of cruel jokes, and I was always the punch line.

My father, Dan Worthington, was convicted for the robbery and attempted homicide of Ruby Parker, a lonely widow with too much money and not enough sense to get a home security system. While my father claims he didn't do it, who can believe him? He's spent a lifetime as a broke drunk. His word is as good as the gold backing up the American dollar. And I'm pretty sure the United States Treasury is bankrupt.

So many thoughts pour through my head. A mixture of hatred and pity. It tastes bittersweet as I bite down on the reality that Dad is probably gone for good. Not because he'll be in the Durham County Detention Facility for the foreseeable future, but because of his own personal prison that he'll never escape. He never even tried to be a father as he drank his life away, and now we'll both grow older and further apart.

I cling to a subtle sense of realization that I will miss bygone days, as crappy as they were, but I put that nostalgia on the backburner.

A thought haunts me. What will my life become? What is my finish line? I didn't crouch at the same starting line as everyone else. I'm a mess. I need a father. I want to be happy, to be at peace. I want to stop loving, stop needing, stop reaching for something to hold me above water and instead tread for myself. Yet I'm too tired to keep paddling against the current.

I watched my father break down at the conclusion of his trial. Tears streamed down his face and convulsions shook his thick body as I watched his soul shatter. It was the epitome of hopelessness. I will always remember that moment because it touched me so deeply in a way I've never experienced. Raw emotion. Perhaps it was the culmination of my sister's murder and Dad's conviction—desperation at its darkest.

I fear that with Dad's sentencing I will become a blip on Fate's screen, much like many who come and go in our lives, passing life by in a haze. Will Dad even think of me while he's gone? I'm his only son, his firstborn, and somehow I've already been forgotten—a father-son connection that lasted a fleeting moment at my birth, then grew too tiresome for him to maintain. It hurts so much to love another person and then let them go. Suffering—is it inevitable with all relationships in life? The constant sifting of people, an ever-changing tide of hopeless relationships...?

Perhaps everything is pointless and bleak. If my father indeed didn't do the crime as he claims, justice is a farce. And if he did, trust is worthless. What is there to live for if nothing and no one can be counted on?

Maybe one day I'll find out. But today isn't that day.

Chapter 1

The day that Mia Germaine ambled into my wreck of a life stretched into the most beautiful tragedy I would ever experience—if only it hadn't required a blood sacrifice. The life of one I loved murdered at the hands of one I hated.

It all started with death, and ended with death. My own sister, Alexis Worthington, was a too-young life snuffed out before her time. No prom dress shopping to max out Mom's credit card. No getting wasted at her high school graduation party and regretting it. No "finding herself" at college. No husband to fight with. No kids to spoil. No regrets to enjoy and survive.

Alexis's life boiled down to a meager turnout at a poor man's funeral where even the post-ceremony snacks came out of a generic Ritz Crackers box. After twenty-two years being six feet under in the funeral home's cheapest box, Alexis was a rag-shrouded pile of dust by now. Meanwhile, my own perpetual rot continued daily.

Worms of regret wriggled through my core. Parasites of depression bit at my flesh. I was always a moment away from becoming a soulless carcass—until Mia Germaine came along.

Nothing could quell the devastation that shattered me into pieces of a man I no longer recognized... except for love.

Me, Landon Worthington—a man who survived without love my entire childhood—would come to know love with such intimacy even Shakespeare couldn't find words to describe it. I never understood it until Mia's arrival on my doorstep. It was not a romantic infatuation with something shiny and pretty dangling in front of my face, lingering at my fingertips. Not a burning passion that sets sheets on fire. No, it was something so much deeper, much purer. A familiar embrace from someone whose heart you possess, and who possesses your own for eternity.

Few ever experience this kind of love. It takes more than a grand gesture to feel it.

It takes something extraordinary. Something bigger than me, bigger than you, bigger than life.

It's salvation.

Mia *did* save my life, after all.

It was a shame she couldn't save every part of me, the worst parts of me.

Some people leave footprints that wash away from the ebb and flow of life, while others cement them as a permanent reminder that they touched you in some meaningful way. Mia's tracks, while heavy and burdened with her own suffering, welcomingly stomped all over me, leaving in their prints puddles of hope where before there was none.

I had witnessed too much death, too much pain for one soul to bear, but Mia washed it all away with a question that spurred an investigation that would not only capture a killer, but also free an innocent:

"Do you think he really did it?"

The query about my father's conviction from two decades earlier challenged my own beliefs to the core. Was my father innocent of his crimes?

Until Mia came along, I never had the balls to find out. She gave me the heart I needed to press for answers.

But this isn't a love story. Not the conventional kind, anyway. This is a story of friendship. Only the beginning of one, for now. It's a story of recovering from loss, finding yourself amid tragedy, and clinging to that lifesaver when it's tossed to you in the storm.

I never gave up, even though I did eventually give in. Give in to what, you ask? Give in to the gift that Mia gave me. Together we would conquer our demons and rise from the wreckage of our mutual suffering. A father and son reconciled, and a victim's eternal silence broken at last.

I'll warn you now that you aren't going to get all the answers about my sister's murder here. Not yet, at least. That's a different tale, one that only Mia can tell.

But you *will* get answers about how it all started, and how the bigger picture ends.

While my brokenness started after Alexis's murder in March of 1992, salvation was only twenty-two years behind it...

Chapter 2

Whoever says crime doesn't pay has never been on the receiving end of the barrel of a gun. For Derek Worthington, crime was his only salvation today—his escape from certain death. He needed cash, and he needed it yesterday. And no one in his position came by that kind of cash without some kind of criminal activity.

As the face of the man holding the weapon blurred into a hazy shadow beyond, all Derek could focus on was the black muzzle eyeing him, daring him to move.

Luckily he wasn't willing to take that dare.

With 250 pounds of force behind him, Fivehead—his nickname on the streets, but never to his face, due to the long slope of his forehead that you could project a movie on—had barged through Derek's front door only moments ago with a thirst for blood. Specifically *Derek's* blood. Derek had only seen Fivehead's face once before, and he had hoped to never see it again.

That hope had proved promising... until today.

"So da boss tells me to come down here and shake some sense into ya, Worthington. But from what I see, I don't think ya got none." Fivehead scowled at the shambles that Derek called a home. A draft from the kitchen reeked of molding leftovers, and the floors looked like they hadn't seen a vacuum this century. "I'm wondering if you're worth more dead than alive."

"Please... don't kill me," Derek begged.

Images of his brains splattered across the peeling dandelion-yellow wallpaper flashed across his mind. In this horrific vision, a jagged hole gaped across the back of his head, edged by blood-matted brown hair and chunks of dandruff. The puke-green carpet sprinkled with red, the corduroy sofa stained with gray matter, his body in a lifeless heap on the floor.

The visuals were too much to stomach.

Derek felt a wetness slither down his leg, puddling at his feet. Not his proudest moment.

Apparently the expanding damp spot on his trousers caught Fivehead's eye as he cruelly smirked, then laughed.

"Man up, Derek. Afraid of a piece of metal?" Fivehead waved the gun at Derek, then resumed his steady aim.

"I don't wanna die!" Derek sobbed.

"Ya know why I'm here," Fivehead's gravelly voice continued, not an inkling of mercy tingeing his words. "Tell me why I shouldn't kill ya right now."

"I can get the money. Ya know I'm good for it. I just need time."

"Good for it?" Fivehead snorted. "You're good for nothin', man. Boss ain't happy to find out you're late paying up again. If you ain't gonna pay, you ain't gonna play, my friend. You know the rules."

"I'll get ya your money plus interest. I swear. I gotta plan." Derek's vow came out hoarse and trembly, a clear sign of weakness to an enforcer like Fivehead. But then again, the business end of the gun was inching closer to Derek's temple than was comfortable.

Fivehead tapped his chin with his thick index finger, his smile a riddle that Derek couldn't solve. Either Fivehead would give him a second chance or kill him, and he was taking his time deciding. It was a psychological game of Russian roulette, but unfortunately Derek wasn't holding the gun. Fivehead was.

"I'll tell ya what. I'm a nice guy. I'll give you one week. *One week*," Fivehead emphasized. "But if you have another excuse for me, I'm first goin' after ya family so you can watch, then you're next. And I assure you, my friend, no excuse will cut it."

"I gotcha, man. You won't be sorry. I'll have it all for ya."

"You better, or this will be the last thing you see." Fivehead jabbed his pistol into Derek's forehead, leaving a circular brand on his skin in case Derek questioned his sincerity.

Derek believed the threat with all his cowardly heart. He knew Fivehead had killed before and would do it again without batting an eyelash. The only question was who would go first—his brother Dan? His sister-in-law Jennifer? His niece Alexis? His nephew Landon? That was the only family he had, and while he didn't want to die at Fivehead's hand, if he put his family in harm's way, his brother would do a lot worse to him.

Just as Fivehead turned to leave, he swung back around, his arm outstretched and aimed right at Derek's head. Suddenly Derek felt the crack of metal against his skull, then blackness.

What seemed like moments later, Derek blinked back to consciousness on the threadbare living room carpet in a prostrate heap of achy joints. As his eyes adjusted to the dim light of a 40-watt bulb perched crookedly in a shade-less lamp, he rubbed his throbbing temples. Then total recall kicked in.

He had one week to come up with ten thousand dollars, or else he was a dead man walking.

Chapter 3

2014
Thursday, May 8

Restless nights are some of the most eloquent nights. Although ruthless, it is in the darkness where the soul murmurs sweet nothings to our fears, quelling them if only for a moment, then rousing them with new vigor. Nightfall is a time of reflection, of mourning, of yearning, of hoping, of seething. It's in those loneliest of eves when truth reveals itself, showing its face from behind a mask of lies.

I had lived my fair share of lies. But there was only one person I trusted enough with the truth.

Mia.

I knew I could tell her everything, and *would* tell her everything. In due time.

Only, I had spoken what I felt today and now regretted the aftermath. It started with a phone call... and ended with an argument.

"I don't have proof or anything, but I'm not so sure your dad's the one who should be behind bars," Mia had speculated over the phone earlier that day. And for some reason her defense of my jerk father pissed me off.

Why, you may ask? Because he abandoned our family, emotionally abused us for years, and may as well have left us for dead. He was the reason my sister was killed, and he was the reason my life could never be resurrected from the ashes. Thanks to Dad, I stopped believing in phoenixes years ago.

As the recall of my conversation with Mia replayed in my head, my thoughts turned more grisly. Suffering hadn't only preyed on my family, but on all of humanity. Doom circled above, like a vulture zeroing in on a carcass, delighting in its decay.

Lying on my bed, I closed my eyes, still envisioning that vulture's descent. Perhaps sleep had descended as well, because when my cell phone chirped me awake, it was 5:53 a.m.

I instantly knew who was calling. But I didn't know why.

"Mia Germaine... two calls in one night. What now?" I grumbled, letting my voice convey just how perturbed I was over the abrupt way our last conversation had ended.

Silence. Then a meek voice rose across the vacant space. "I wanted to apologize... for everything. How can I make it up to you?"

"You know my answer to that," I stated matter-of-factly, a crooked grin creasing my lips.

Our phone call not even an hour earlier had concluded on a sour note and a hang-up, so when Mia offered the peace pipe, I was ready to smoke it.

"Beer and pizza?" she gambled tentatively.

"You know me so well," I replied.

After she arrived at my house a few minutes later, we talked toppings and brews for several minutes, until the topic meandered to what caused our earlier dissension—whether my father had indeed robbed a house and wounded the resident, a crime he vehemently denied committing. I led the way down this conversational path.

"I've been thinking a lot about it, and I'm starting to wonder about my dad's involvement."

"So do you think he did it?" she asked point-blank, her hazel eyes wide and penetrating.

It was an unvoiced question I had pondered many times over the years, eventually leading me to the conclusion that of course he did. He was a selfish ass, so why wouldn't he have done it? But today my convictions swept that logic aside. I just didn't know anymore.

"Maybe I should ask him. If he says he didn't, I want to believe him. And if he admits to all of his other sins, why lie about this?"

"True."

"But then on the flip side," I resumed, playing devil's advocate against my own mind, "I have to ask on what grounds could they convict him if he was innocent? Surely the evidence must have pointed to him to land him in jail."

"Except that they convict innocent people all the time."

I sighed. "What does it matter? I hardly know the man. Why should I care?"

"Because he's your dad. I would give anything to see my dad again."

A pang of guilt tapped me with its bony finger. Mia had lost her father in a car accident around the same time mine went to jail. While we both lost our fathers that year, at least mine was a jail visit away. Six feet of dirt separated Mia from hers, leaving her with only an austere headstone to connect with. Perhaps my situation wasn't as bad as it felt some days.

"Maybe you're right. Though, how will I know if he's telling me the truth? I don't know how to tell the truth from the lies."

"Maybe that's not your job, Landon. Just hear him out. Then once you have his side, put on your mental gardening gloves and dig deeper to find out the truth."

"Real men don't wear gardening gloves," I retorted.

She nudged me lightly with her shoulder and laughed. "Whatever. You know what I'm trying to say. Maybe your job is simply to listen to your heart."

It sounded simple enough, or like a cheesy 1980's song. But my heart had long ago stopped talking.

"And what if my heart has nothing to say about it?" I asked her, knowing she'd have an answer for any question I tossed at her.

She thought for a moment, then shrugged. "Then you go all Bonnie Raitt on it and 'give it something to talk about... a little mystery to figure out.'"

A SECONDHAND LIE

When a second later she broke into song, I knew it was going to be an interesting day.

❧❧

Durham County Detention Facility
Later that day...

As my footsteps echoed along the painted concrete floor, I mentally prepared myself for lies. Firsthand lies from my dad about how much he loved his family but regretted not being a better father. Secondhand lies from my mom about how much Dad wished he could fix things between us. And then there were all the lies in between.

Today was the first time in twenty-two years that I mustered the courage to visit my father, Dan Worthington, alone. Only once before had I come—and that was a month ago with Mia's prodding and emotional support. My reasons for that previous visit rested solely on finding my sister's killer, but today it was about my relationship with my dad. So here I was, by myself in a roomful of killers and thieves, and my own flesh and blood was among them.

I felt eyes scouring me, ears eavesdropping. Jail wasn't a place for pretty boys like me, with my clean-shaven face and gelled Salon Blu haircut. Tense jaws clenched as I passed vestibules where cartoonishly over-muscled criminals flexed arms thicker than my thigh. Eyes that had caused and relished violence watched me with malice. Hard faces crinkled with curiosity—and some, I shuddered to realize, with desire. I felt like an endangered species on display—vulnerable, ready to flee, and wanting never to return.

But I couldn't run yet. I hadn't gotten what I came for.

The truth.

The metal chair groaned and squeaked as I sat down, resting my arms stiffly on the cold table. My nerves were snapping with anxiety about what I would ask, how Dad

13

would answer, and what unspoken confessions lingered between the lines.

Two minutes into my wait, a guard led my father—dressed in a loose, faded green jumpsuit that shrunk the man within it—to the chair in front of me. I exhaled the pent-up energy that had surfaced through the tapping of my foot on the floor.

As Dad sat down, he seemed smaller than I remembered. He had always been a towering figure—even to me, at a lean six-foot-two. Although bulky from years of prison workouts, I assumed, there was something meek about his bearing.

"Hey, Landon," Dad said with a genuine smile. "It's great to see you again so soon. I wasn't sure if you'd ever come back."

"I wasn't planning on it," I replied tersely.

"Can't say I blame you." Turning his neck right and left, Dad scanned the room. "Where's your friend—Mia?"

"She didn't come with me this time. It's just me... me and you."

Dad sighed in what I could only interpret as relief. "I'm glad. I kinda wanted to talk to you man-to-man one of these days. I just didn't expect it to be today."

"There's no better time than now, right?" Clichés were all I could afford. My own words were buried too deep to surface.

"Yep, that's true." He paused. "You look good, son. A little tired, though. You doin' okay?"

"I'm fine. What did you want to talk about?" I wondered aloud, itching to move the idle chitchat along.

For a long moment he said nothing, only examined me. His liver-spotted hand, roughened by time, reached out to me, touched the heavily smudged Plexiglas pane that separated us halfway across the table, then returned to his lap. When his gaze shifted downward, I noticed pools of swelling emotion in his eyes. For a second I mistook it for a smudge on the glass, until he blinked the teardrop free. The droplet coursed its way down his cheek, then dropped into the oblivion below.

"It's funny. I, uh... I've had two decades to plan for this moment, and when it arrives I'm speechless. I don't even know where to begin."

Dad wiped at his watering eyes, his lips quivering. With an unconscious gesture, he ran his palm over his balding head.

It was the rawest emotion I'd ever witnessed from him... other than the day of his conviction.

"There's no starting place for an apology, I suppose," he continued. "You just dive in the middle."

As I watched this hardened man break, suddenly the anger and hurt and frustration and neglect I'd accumulated over a lifetime of letdowns lifted, and in its stead was pity. I pitied my father for being trapped in his own poor decisions, left in a piss-reeking crypt to rot for mistakes that had arisen from bad decision after bad decision. Looking at him now, I knew he wasn't evil to the core. Just broken. Like me.

"Dad, you can talk to me. What do you want to tell me? Now's your chance." Although the words sounded clipped, there was heart attached to them.

"First, that I'm sorry. I'm sorry I spent more nights at the bar than with you. Sorry that I drove your mom into the arms of other men. Sorry that Alexis died because I wasn't there to protect her. Sorry for it all." He stopped, but when I opened my mouth to speak—what, I wasn't even sure yet—his meaty palm shot up.

"Son, I'm paying the price for my sins, and I want you to know I don't see myself as a victim of circumstance or none of that bullshit that some of these guys in here feel. I didn't take care of you and your sister like I should have. I didn't love your mother like she deserved. You all were innocent, and I ruined you with my selfishness. Drinking and wasting away the only good things I got in life—you, Alexis, and your mom. I wish—"

Dad's voice halted as a sob escaped, and for the second time in my life I saw my father cry. Not a watered-down version of sadness, but heartbreaking, soul-crushing bawling. "I wish you could have had better. I'm sorry, son, that you got stuck with a lousy father."

If only a wall of Plexiglas didn't separate us, I would have hugged him. Squeezed him with all the love that had been missing for two decades, restoring all that was lost in that one healing embrace. I needed it. He needed it. We both needed it after all we had suffered through since the day Alexis was murdered.

"Dad, I've forgiven you for everything." It was little consolation for the torment he was clearly feeling, but it was all I could offer.

"Oh, Landon, there's not enough forgiveness in the world to wipe away what I've done. Your sister's dead cuz of me. Your mother, well, I made her life a living hell. And you—God only knows the damage I've done there. Ain't no forgiveness enough, son."

Part of me agreed with him. He left lives in ruin behind his acts of carelessness. But he had spent years paying for it, and by now it should have been paid in full. Then I wondered, was jail even enough? Enough to cover the cost of Alexis's life?

"As corny as it sounds, I figure you've just about paid your debt to society by now," I said, trying to console him.

"Yep, one of life's little ironies," he muttered with a chuckle.

"What do you mean?" I asked.

"Just that I got put in here for a crime I didn't do, but I deserved much worse, I'd say. It's just ironic is all. But I guess that's karma for ya."

"So you're sticking to the story that you didn't rob that lady's house or shoot her or have anything to do with it?"

Dad shook his head. "I swear, I've done a lot of bad things, but that wasn't one of them. In fact, while the robbery was going on, I was buying a bouquet of gas station roses, then waiting for your mother to get home to surprise her. It's no matter. I'm getting my just deserts."

Just deserts or not, if my dad was telling the truth—and I admittedly still had my doubts—whoever *did* do the crime got away with it. That wasn't justice at all.

"Dad, you shouldn't be in jail for a crime you didn't commit. Do you know who *was* involved?"

"I have my suspicions, but it ain't worth doing anything about."

"Tell me," I insisted with a firmness that left him no alternative. "I want to know exactly what happened."

"Why dig it up now, after all this time?"

"Because the real offender got off the hook because he baited you. Justice isn't about catching *a* criminal, but catching *the* criminal. Dad, if you didn't do it, someone else did. And his actions warrant punishment. Do you know who was involved?" I repeated.

I heard a symphony of tiny crackles as my dad rolled the kinks out of his beefy neck. "Well, at first I thought it was your Uncle Derek. But I just don't think your uncle could have done it alone. Besides him, there was only one other guy who knew about it—we called him Grizzle, but his real name was Gene. But I dunno...I don't think it was him neither."

"Those were the only two who knew about it—and you can for sure rule them out?"

"I can't for sure say both was innocent, but as far as I know they were."

I needed more info if I was going to figure this out. "Tell me everything from the beginning, Dad. Every detail you can recall."

"You got time?" Dad asked, glancing at a dirty-faced clock in a wire cage above the exit.

"As much time as it takes."

"Well, it all started when your Uncle Derek got himself sucked into some shady business and dragged me down with him..."

And thus began the story of how my dad and I set ourselves free.

Chapter 4

1992
All People's Grill
Durham, North Carolina

The black-and-white-checkered tile disguised the scuffmarks from years of patrons Jitterbugging to the live roadhouse blues combos that often took to the stage. Only a handful of people were out on a Wednesday night at this hour, talking over the lull of B.B. King's "The Thrill Is Gone" that swept throughout the small three-room establishment. Like all the best BBQ joints, it didn't look like much from the outside— just a plain, two-toned concrete block affair, with a gravel-and-dirt parking lot that would have been at home on any country road in the South. The locals—and lucky travelers— revered it for the best chicken 'cue anywhere, bar none.

At a wooden table pushed against a corner of the main room, brothers Dan and Derek Worthington sat on one side, mirror images of each other in their yellowed Hanes t-shirts, while a man with a frizzy, dirty white beard known as "Grizzle" lounged opposite them smoking a Marlboro and nursing a Budweiser bottle.

"What's so urgent you needed to drag me from the middle of my poker game?" Dan grumbled at his brother after he tossed back a shot of Wild Turkey. "I was gonna win big tonight, I could feel it."

"Forget poker. You'll never git ahead. Naw, I got a lead on how we can git our hands on some money... *big* money, brother." Derek smiled crookedly, his overcrowded teeth a dull yellow-brown from years of tobacco and black coffee.

"Big money, you say? Sounds shady to me," Dan said with a shake of his head. "I'm not into anything that's gonna git me arrested. I'm tryin' to fix things up with my family, ya know."

"Fixin' things? You're crazy if ya think Jennifer's goin' back to you." At this Derek cackled loud enough to wrest the attention from a girl at the bar wearing neon print biker shorts with a hot-pink cropped tank top revealing an inappropriate glimpse of her under-boob. Her permed hair stood tall and stiff under a pound of hairspray as she turned back to her friends. Derek's lips curled in a lusty grin.

As Derek ogled her a little too long, the boyfriend attached to her bare waist turned and glared. Setting his glass of dark beer down, he rose from his stool, his high-top fade haircut and LA Gear sneakers adding at least two more inches to his already impressive six feet four inches. Yet Derek refused to cower, maintaining his challenge.

The younger man slowly removed his colorblock Nike windbreaker, one sleeve then the other with dramatic bravado—the universal sign for *let's take it outside.*

Dan grabbed Derek's shoulder and swung him around to face him. "Will you stop it? Every peckerwood in here is giving us the stink-eye. Back down, cuz I ain't backing you up tonight."

Tossing a nonverbal plea to their so-far silent companion, Derek got another refusal for aid. "I ain't part of this," Grizzle said, kicking his booted feet up on an empty chair. "You on your own, Derek."

His cockiness subsiding now that he was going solo, Derek withdrew with two raised palms of surrender. "Sorry, man. I wasn't meaning no harm."

The young man tilted his chin up in victory, then turned back to his posse.

"You better git to the point before we git kicked outta here," Grizzle urged as he finished off his last swig of beer.

"Right, as I was sayin', I know a way for us to make a load of cash. Quick, too. Alls it takes is a little recon, which is what Dan's for. The rest me and Grizzle'll handle."

"Me? What do I know about reconnaissance? I don't even wanna be a part of it."

Derek closed his eyes in frustration, thrust his head back, and tightened his lips. After a calming breath, he looked his brother square in the eyes. "Do ya want your wife back?"

"Yeah," Dan replied. "Course I do."

"Then you gotta make a grand gesture. Valentine's is comin' up. Gitter sumpthin' nice. Spoil the kids for once. Use the money to catch up on bills. Shit, I don't care what you do with it, but this is our chance—*your* chance—to get on top. You either grab this opportunity, or ya lose everything. Which'll it be?"

Dan humphed, then rolled his eyes. "Tell me more about this supposed opportunity," he said with a groan.

"Well, ya know all them fancy houses in that subdivision off of 157, near that church?"

"Yeah," Dan said warily.

"There's an old lady who used to live in one of them mini mansions, but word is that her daughter sent her to a nursing home type place. All her stuff's just sitting there, waiting to be auctioned off or donated to charity, unless we get there first—"

"Hold up," Dan whispered harshly. "Your plan is to rob an old lady?"

"No... my plan is to empty out a mansion that no one lives in."

With a thrust against the back slats of his seat, Dan let out a staccato "ha ha!" before leaning in closely. "You're kidding, right? Derek, I ain't gonna rob nobody. I admit I'm not a good guy, but I'm not a bad guy either. And what you're talking about isn't right. We're gonna get caught, and we're gonna go to jail. All for what? A few hundred bucks? No way, man. You gotta come up with something better than this."

With childlike exuberance, Derek shuffled his chair closer, the excitement of his words building. "Don't ya see? It doesn't get better than this. This lady was loaded. And her daughter is just tossing her stuff out. It's a victimless crime. Just look into it, Dan. I'll give ya the street name and number. Check it out, and if it ain't what I'm telling you, then fine—we'll call it off. But if it is what I'm sayin', we have all the world to gain. And we can git it done next Friday night. In and out and over. I'm sure Jennifer would love a new TV, and the kids could use new clothes, right?"

Amid the promise of wealth and new beginnings, something wasn't being said, and Dan knew it. Scratching his chin, he eyed his seedy brother, wondering what he was leaving out. "Why you so eager to do this so soon? Why not wait a little, think this through?"

"We can't wait or else the stuff'll be gone," Derek said, spraying the table with spittle in his fluster. "We gotta do this now. It's an open door; let's walk through. Please, don't let me down," Derek entreated, his worry pleating folds along his forehead where his hairline was just starting to recede.

Dan hadn't seen such passion from Derek since he was a kid begging Mom for the latest GI Joe figure—back when they were a measly $2.32 each. Well, that and the Satellite Jumping Shoes, which Mom immediately nixed since ten-year-old Derek wasn't known for his coordination.

So clearly Derek was in trouble. He was never the "idea man" in the group. He was a sheep, one that always got stuck in the briars. Something was up, and Derek apparently needed cash fast. And if Derek was indeed in trouble, that meant Dan's own family could be on someone's shit list too. There was only one choice to make.

Dan rubbed his hand along his neck, then warily agreed. "I guess I'll look into it and see what I find out. But you gotta be honest with me, Derek. Is there anything you ain't telling me?"

"Nah, man. Just that I need money, you need money, we all need money—and this is how we can score it quick." Next Derek turned his attention to Grizzle. "And you—I already know you're in, right?"

"Hell yeah. I could use the cash," was all it took to put the ball in motion.

Each of the brothers had high stakes at risk—Dan, his family, and Derek, his life—but only one would end up losing both.

Chapter 5

2014
Friday, May 9

When a man admits vulnerability, he instantly becomes less of a man. At least that's what my father had always taught me. Until now.

Vulnerability had instead become my warrior's sword as I slashed through years of harbored secrets. Although thirty-eight years too late to save our family, I vowed to join my father as a team where I hoped we would someday cut the ribbon at the finish line that would lead us toward a better future.

Lies were a sin of the past, Dad assured me. And trust was a promise of the future.

I clung to this as I headed to the Durham Police Station to visit my long-time friend, Evan Williams—*Detective Williams*, he made me call him when trying to impress his peers. His request always provoked the opposite response from me, however. Something along the lines of *Dickhead* Williams, which he never saw the humor in.

So much for my wit.

With a sense of familiarity I wove through the clusters of cubicles and found Evan sitting behind a stack of files, leafing through an especially thick folder. When I strode up to him, casting a shadow on his hunched form, he hurriedly closed the file in a tight grip. Clearly whatever he was reading was top secret. As he greeted me, I watched his fingers push the file under the stack, out of sight of my probing eyes.

"Hey, bro. Got a question for you," I began.

"You and your questions always get me in trouble," Evan groused, heaving a weary sigh. "What do you need?"

Now that I was here, I wasn't sure what I was looking for. Some kind of evidence that would prove my father's innocence. But what could do that... especially two decades after the fact?

"How difficult would it be to access a police report from twenty years ago... like, from my dad's arrest?"

"Easy. It wasn't the Dark Ages, Lan. They were electronically filed back in the 1990s. Should only take me a minute to retrieve it. What are you looking into that for? Does it have something to do with your sister's murder?"

As Alexis's murder was still an ongoing cold case investigation, Evan—the only one in the department who seemed to care after so many years—still looked into every possible angle that could lead to her killer. I didn't know if the home robbery was affiliated in any way or a worthwhile lead to pursue, but considering the close timeline, anything was possible.

"I'm not sure if it's related or not, but since the robbery happened barely a month before her death, and it involved some nefarious people, maybe it's connected?"

"Sounds like a far reach," Evan said, his doubt swatting my hopes aside.

Regardless of his skepticism, his fingers dashed along the keyboard, paused, then he waved me over to his side of the desk. I skimmed the monitor. An arrest report for my father revealed all of the facts about the crime:

Date of incident: February 12, 1992
Time: Wednesday evening, around 11 p.m.
Suspect Name: Daniel Landon Worthington
Age: 36
Marital Status: Married
Hair Color: Brown
Eye Color: Brown
Race: Caucasian
Height: 6'2"
Victim: Ruby Parker

A SECONDHAND LIE

Witnesses: Robert Dillon (neighbor)

Crime committed: armed residential robbery and aggravated assault

Details: The victim was at home sleeping when she woke up to the sound of breaking glass on the first floor. When she went downstairs, a tall man, approximately 6 feet tall, wearing a black mask, pointed a gun at her using his right hand and told her not to scream. As she turned to run, a shot rang out and the victim was struck in the back of her shoulder by a bullet. The perpetrator fled the scene, but she was able to reach the phone to call 9-1-1. Due to the age of the victim and severe blood loss, the injury turned out to be life-threatening. One shot was fired, based on the recovery of only one shell casing at the scene, a .38 Special. According to eyewitness testimony by the neighbor, Robert Dillon, he was asleep in his home next door when he heard a shot fired. He looked out the window and saw a masked intruder flee the house, get into a brown, early-model coupe, and drive away. He was unable to see the license plate number, but guessed the make and model of the getaway vehicle to be an early 1980s Ford Tempo. Other neighbors were questioned, and all recalled the single gunshot, but none saw anything or anyone.

Disposition: An anonymous tip called in on Thursday, February 13, 1992, claimed Daniel Worthington was responsible for the robbery. When vehicle registration records were pulled, the make and model matched a vehicle registered to Worthington, a 1984 brown Ford Tempo coupe. The physical description also fit.

As I read the incident report, my first question was who the getaway driver could be. If my dad's certainty that Uncle Derek and this Grizzle guy weren't involved proved true, that left me with nothing. My second question was who reported the anonymous tip. A hunch told me that the same person who called in the tip would lead me to the perpetrator's front door.

"Did they do ballistics to match the bullet to a particular gun?" I asked, reaching for any possible angle investigators hadn't considered twenty years ago.

"We didn't do gun ballistics back then. We only gathered obvious details based on the shell casing—a .38 Special, which could point to any number of revolvers," Evan explained. "Regardless, the evidence has been long discarded. Since the case was adjudicated with no appeal, we got rid of the evidence years ago. Sorry, Landon. I wish I could give you something more, but for cases as old as this one, there's not much we can do."

No evidence. No leads. Nothing tangible to cling to. Any lingering faith I had deflated like a week-old balloon as the prospect of exonerating my dad grew dimmer. And then there was that nagging question that perpetually loomed: What if my dad wasn't being honest with me?

I was a dog chasing a car on a busy road—futilely pursuing something I'd never catch, and more than likely to get my ass run over in the process.

I knew it was conniving. Sneaky. Distrustful. But I had to do it regardless.

No matter how much I wanted to believe my dad, I simply couldn't do it on blind trust. Trust no one. Not even myself. It was my motto. There was only one way to know for sure whether my dad was telling the truth.

"Mom, you home?" I called out as I walked through her front door. The smell of homemade marinara sauce enveloped me as I walked in, and immediately my salivary glands started working overtime.

"In the kitchen, honey," she replied as I heard metal clinking in the background.

As I rounded the entryway, I noticed the pristine shine of the hardwood floors and slipped off my shoes, leaving them against the wall. A subtle hint of lemon Lysol wafted over me—of course she had dusted too. The woman never rested.

I found her in the kitchen pulling a steaming casserole dish from the oven, and I recognized the layer of melted mozzarella immediately. Lasagna. One of her specialties... though I'd long ago lost tabs on my list of favorite homemade dishes. Over the years Mom had become a goddess in the kitchen—either her way of making up for my childhood of frozen dinners, or a means to pass the time alone and single.

The dinette table on the far end of the kitchen was set for two, a stark reminder that I was all she had. Red wine filled a pair of cheap wine glasses, and a Caesar salad sat in a decorative bowl in the center. A loaf of Italian bread was sliced and waiting next to a ceramic, floral butter dish.

"Dinner's ready, honey," Mom said, gesturing me to sit down as she carried the entrée to the table.

"Before we eat, Mom, I wanted to talk to you about something." I hated to ruin a perfectly fine meal with talk about Dad, but it had to be done. Now. I couldn't wait any longer.

"Sure. What's going on, hon? Everything okay?" A typical worried mother response to my vague request.

"Yeah, everything's fine. I wanted to ask you about the night Dad got charged with that robbery."

Her faltering hands didn't escape my attention as she set the hot pan on a pansy-adorned trivet and swiped at a stray hair across her forehead. Without a word, she waved for me to follow as she headed up to her bedroom on the second story. As she climbed the stairs, I noticed the slight slump in her shoulders, her slow and weary gait, and the way her soft yet wrinkled hands slid up the railing as if releasing it would send her falling into an abyss. Mom was aging, but more than that, she was giving up.

It broke my heart.

We headed into her bedroom, a flowery den with a rose-covered bedspread, matching valances, and a pale pink area rug, all perfectly suited to a woman whose sense of interior design was stuck in the early eighties. Old-fashioned but tasteful and scrupulously clean.

She opened the top dresser drawer where a simple hairbrush and mirror sat, and pulled out a wooden box, then handed it to me.

"What's this?" I asked.

"Open it," she urged.

So I did.

A small bronze clasp held the box shut, and after fiddling with it for a moment, I lifted the lid. Inside I discovered a stack of letters and a single rose, ancient and dried but intact, its once vibrant red now darkened into an ancient burgundy. The trace scent of vanilla emanated from the notes within as my fingertips gingerly flipped through the contents. Attached to the rose was a card.

"Read it," Mom said, pointing to the card.

I pulled the aged card out, the fragrance of timeless memories captured on yellowed parchment wafting upward. It was a haunting sensation, delving into my mother's musty secrets while she watched over my shoulder.

"To my beautiful wife, Jenny," I read aloud from handwriting I recognized.

I know I'm not the man you deserve, but give me a chance to become him. I want to give you the life we've always dreamed of, the family we always talked about, the fulfilled hopes we always clung to. I love you, darling, and I want to fix what I've broken. Please let me prove my worth to you.

Love always, Dan

Below my father's name was a date:

February 12, 1992.

The day of the robbery.

Dad was indeed buying flowers for my mom the same night he was supposedly robbing a place? It didn't sound logical, even to the most cynical of skeptics—me.

So he wasn't lying after all.

"Your father camped outside the front door holding a bouquet of flowers and this card the night of the robbery. He waited and waited for me to answer the door, but I had been drinking and was acting belligerent, until I finally sent him away sometime after one in the morning. Poor guy couldn't even leave with some dignity because of that damn car stalling out. Took over ten minutes for him to finally get it started."

We both chuckled at recalling Dad's infamous Ford Tempo and the god-awful sound it made, like a yowling cat with a smoker's cough, whenever he tried to crank it. Not once did it ever start right up, and it was a toss-up whether that or the car's hideous color, a sickly turd brown, was the bigger embarrassment.

"I never told you this, but there was no way he could have been part of that robbery, because he was sitting right outside the entire evening—for hours. He was that determined to win me back," she said, a hint of a smile playing upon her lips.

I watched the reminiscence capture her, drawing her into a moment that only she intimately knew and could

29

appreciate—the undying love and fortitude of her long-lost husband pursuing her with everything he had.

"You let Dad go to jail for something he didn't do? Why?"

"At the time I wanted nothing more than for him to do time. I needed to get away from him. After losing your sister, I blamed him. He hadn't protected her, and I heaped the fault on his shoulders. I was so angry, Landon."

"But you could have said something to the cops to help him, Mom!" I yelled, frustrated at her part in dissolving our family.

"I just... couldn't let him stay in my life, Landon. He was toxic. You wouldn't understand. Besides, it wouldn't have mattered. No cop would have believed me back then. My reputation was, well, less than credible at that point in my life. Plus your father strongly felt that I should let him go, that I'd be better off without him. He also believed he deserved jail for his sins... the ones you don't know about and don't need to know about. Please forgive us, but we did what we needed to do. And we're okay now. It's not ideal, but we've moved past it. So should you."

No words could describe the rush of emotions sucking me into their depths—anger, betrayal... and resolution.

Maybe she was right. They did what they felt was right, and I couldn't possibly understand the why behind it. Regardless, Mom still trusted him after all those years of neglect, forgave him for all the devastation he left in his wake. So why couldn't I? What bitterness was I clinging to, harboring in my heart so protectively that I was willing to let my father pay for a crime he didn't commit?

I knew all I needed to know.

Now I just needed to prove it.

"Come on, Landon, food's getting cold," Mom said.

I had forgotten all about dinner. But suddenly I was ravenously hungry.

Chapter 6

The knock on Derek's front door jarred him awake from his slumber on the sofa, immediately putting him in a nasty mood. The interruption pulled him out of a lusty dream from a *Baywatch* scene—his closet television vice. The latest addition to the cast, a busty blonde named Kelly Packard, was spilling cleavage out of her red one-piece swimsuit while hovering over him, oiling him down on a deserted California beach... when a set of knuckles on wood stopped her mid-rub.

Derek squeezed his eyes shut and willed her to straddle him, conjuring the sand, the ocean, the hot babe to return.

But the knocking persisted. So he got up, ready to kill.

Cursing all the way to the front door, he barely cracked it open when Dan bowled through him.

"What are you thinkin', man? The deal is off!" Dan yelled, giving Derek little time to pull his thoughts off of Kelly and on to reality.

"Whatcha talkin' bout?" Derek asked hazily.

"Uh, this Friday, ya idiot. I'm callin' it off."

"Why? What happened?" Derek rubbed his eyes clear of the caked eye goo and reached for a day-old half cup of black coffee on the floor, downing it in one gulp, grimacing.

"You never mentioned she has a gun. Or that she still lives there. Where'd you get your info, anyways? Looks like you've been set up."

Shaking his head, Derek struggled to comprehend what his brother was saying. "A gun? What the shit! What'd you see?"

"I was parking out front this morning, just to get a feel for the neighborhood and all. Sure, fancy houses and rich cars. I'm taking mental inventory of the layout, seeing where we could break in undetected. So there I am, watching the house, when I see an old lady walk right out the front door. So I'm thinking to myself, *Okay, she wasn't moved out after all.* But that's not all. Next I see her pull a handgun—a *gun*, Derek!—out of her purse to check the safety. She was real discreet about it, but I know what I saw. I don't even own no gun, and here's an old lady packing heat! And you're about to send us in there to get ourselves killed? Are you crazy?"

Feeling the heat rising off his brother, Derek tossed his hands up, hoping to defuse his anger. "I swear I had no idea. A buddy of mine gave me the details. He must not 've known," Derek insisted, knowing it was better to be vague about his source. "But... but ya sure you wanna call it off?"

Dan's eyes widened with shock. "Hell yeah I wanna call it off! I'm not bustin' into a house with a bull's-eye on my chest. And neither are you."

"Lemme talk to Grizzle first and see what he thinks. Maybe you were scopin' the wrong house."

"Whatever, man. I'm out of it. Do what you want, but I'm warning you that you're gonna git yourself killed if you step foot in that place."

As Dan turned to leave, Derek touched his arm. "I need to tell ya something before you go."

Derek noticed Dan's clenched knuckles whitening as he slowly turned to face him. Derek was about to get knocked out, but he didn't care. Family was at stake.

"So tell me," Dan seethed.

"What if I told ya that something bigger was at stake?" Derek's words came out in a quiver.

"Bigger—like how big?"

"Like if we don't do this job someone might hurt Jennifer, or Alexis."

No words were angry enough to surface. Just silence—a staggering, timeless hush. Knowledge was written on Dan's weary face. Clearly he had suspected something like this.

Then a sentence. A solitary statement that could make all the troubles go away. "Who, and how much? And when do you need it by?"

"A loan shark I borrowed from. Ten grand. And I need it this week."

Dan nodded weakly. "I'll figure it out. Until then, talk to no one, go nowhere, and stay out of trouble. You risk my family's life again, Derek, and I'll kill you myself."

The front door shook as Dan slammed it closed behind his heavy steps, leaving Derek to wrestle with warring inner voices. The voices often rattled him with their incessant blabbering, rarely coming to an agreement.

Why's Dan always gotta rescue you, you coward? You can't even take care of things yourself.

But it's not my fault. I had things under control, until Dan screwed it up.

Always gotta have big brother bail you out. You're nothing but a failure.

But what alternative was there? Derek didn't have the money. Even if he sold every possession he owned, it wouldn't come close to bringing in the ten grand he owed. He was in it deep this time, with no life jacket to keep him afloat. But the worst part was that Fivehead's threat against his family wasn't empty. Fivehead would just as soon kill a child as squash a bug underfoot. And Derek knew Alexis—his twelve-year-old niece—would be Fivehead's first target, because she was the weakest of them all.

Chapter 7

1992

Ten minutes after Dan's hurried departure, Derek's phone rang. It took a couple loud peals for him to locate the baby blue rotary phone beneath a Chinese food takeout carton where two flies tag-teamed around General Tso's chicken leftovers.

"What?" he spat into the receiver, prepared to hang up on a telemarketer—the only people who seemed to have his number.

"Uncle Derek?" a shy voice asked.

A beat later he recognized it as Alexis. "Yeah, kid, what's up?"

"Can you take me to school today? Mom's out of it." He wondered if his Ford Escort had enough gas. Perhaps a quick detour to pick up Grizzle, then a stop at the gas station on Grizzle's dollar would be worth the trip. He had business to discuss before his big brother took the last tablespoon of dignity from him.

Forty-five minutes later Derek honked outside of 721 Willoughby Way, and Alexis trotted up to the shabby compact car, glancing doubtfully at the nearly bald donut spare on the right front. In the passenger seat sat Grizzle, his wiry beard resting contentedly on his bulging sternum, forcing Alexis to slide into the backseat.

Derek had finished updating Grizzle on the morning's conversation with Dan—excluding the trivial detail of Dan jumping ship—when Alexis shut the door. But despite Derek's confidence that it wasn't something they couldn't handle, Grizzle began voicing his doubts about the whole operation.

"Hey, dude, shut your pie hole," Derek said, nodding over his shoulder at Alexis. "My niece be in the car. We don't talk business with her overhearin', got it?"

"She's just a kid. She don't know nothin'."

Derek spoke in a whisper. "Yeah, well, we don't need her spoutin' on about it, y'know? Besides, I already got everything figured out, and Dan's already got all the details planned."

A small lie ... for now. But Derek figured he'd have time to convince Dan to join them before Grizzle discovered the truth.

The two men fell silent as the car bumped along the asphalt toward the school. For the rest of the ride Derek agonized over how he could convince Grizzle to jump back on board, but with guns involved, maybe it was just best to let Dan take care of things his own way.

As long as this was the last time.

No more messes after this, he vowed. It was time to straighten himself out. Be a man. No more big brother to clean up his messes.

If only it was a promise he could actually keep.

✎✐

Alexis may have only been twelve in years, but she was an old soul.

Perhaps it was a childhood of fending for herself at the hands of neglectful parents that matured her beyond her age. Or the isolation that came with a life of hiding her reality that propelled her to grow up. Some may even argue that a genetic predisposition nurtured her brisk development. Whatever the cause, Alexis was no ordinary twelve-year-old. No, she thought like, felt like, and dreamed like one who had lived a hundred lifetimes imprisoned in misery, yet she still clung to the trust that one day life would be beautiful.

With nomadic wandering, Alexis trudged a lonely path at school. The few friends she clung to throughout elementary school and middle school had transferred out of the ghetto to better school districts, leaving her clique-less and ultimately unseen. Most days felt like a living hell as she watched groups of classmates laughing and bantering and planning after-school fun while she stood on the sidelines. Being shy by nature, Alexis retreated to the vacant shadows, anxiously waiting for the dismissal bell to set her free each afternoon. But once in a while ambling the halls as a transparent ghost of a girl had its perks.

Like overhearing the latest gossip about a playground romance or a classmate's traumatically embarrassing moment. Or watching petty fights over a girl or a "yo' mama" joke. Or today... the revelation of a nasty secret that would put a teacher behind bars.

Mr. Jeremy Mason—the nightmare science teacher with a stick-up-his-ass reputation. Apparently getting an A in his class was like earning a Nobel Prize. Voted least popular teacher among the kids for two years running, Mr. Mason was on a roll to keep this dubious honor as his grading scale grew stricter each year. Perhaps it was because of his youth that he felt the compulsion to prove his worth, but to the students he only proved one thing: He deserved a target on his back.

Alexis had been in the girl's bathroom applying forbidden shades of makeup that her mom warned her would be "advertising stuff to boys that's not on the menu," as she colorfully put it, especially her Madonna-red lipstick. As she was puckering up the finishing touches, a herd of girls noisily bustled in, bumping Alexis aside. The leader of the pack—Renee Clark—was bragging about her latest act of vengeance against her ex-boyfriend.

"Oh my God, I totally kissed Ben, and it made Josh crazy jealous." That was her thing: sending exes into a spiral of envy over her. Somehow the blond beauty knew what made boys tick and tock, which was a puzzle Alexis doubted she'd ever figure out.

The other girls giggled at the admission, which energized the conversation.

"And you know how Mr. Mason gave me a D on my test?" Several mmmhmms later Renee continued, "So, I asked him if he could give me extra credit to bring up my grade and he actually said no, the jerk."

An "oh no he didn't" and "what a jerk" bubbled up from her attentive audience.

"Well, he won't be flunking anyone from now on. I took care of him."

"What'd you do?" a brunette with wire-rimmed glasses and a teased perm asked excitedly. Her pegged acid-washed jeans hung a little too loosely to be fashionable, and her button-up blouse with spaceships was barely cool two years ago. Noting the girl's natural awkwardness, Alexis sensed the poor girl was desperate to fit in with Renee's posse and would do anything for even a slim chance at popularity... even if it meant joining the clique-that-must-not-be-named.

"I told my parents and the principal that he touched me... down there." Renee's gaze drifted down to her crotch, then rose back up to watch her adoring fans' reaction. "He'll never teach again, thanks to me."

"And they believed you?" another girl in preppy Gap khakis asked.

"They have to. It's my word against his, and I'm an innocent kid. Besides, he had it coming. I asked him to let me do extra credit and he said no. I did what I had to."

"Won't he go to jail?" someone whispered.

"I hope so," Renee said with finality. "He deserves whatever he gets. He should've just given me the extra credit."

As Alexis listened to the bathroom confessions continue, she knew this was too important to keep to herself. What she knew about Mr. Mason came mainly from student gossip, but he always waved to her when he drove past her house and was friendly with her mom and their other neighbors. No matter how hard a teacher he was, he didn't deserve prison for something he didn't do. Alexis hoped that by telling her mom she could spare at least one person from Renee Clark's twisted sense of entitlement. There would be many more, Alexis was certain, but to save just one... just one was worth fighting for.

Leaving the cackling hens behind, Alexis headed to her locker wondering when the world had become so dark, and if it was even worth saving.

Chapter 8

Gene Sanders was a formidable son of a gun. The kind of man who makes you lose your faculties with a glare. If I had known what I was up against, I would have never knocked on his door.

After scouring the Internet's public records to find a current address for the nomad, I finally pinpointed a possible residence—an apartment complex on the city's outskirts. Jutting out from the all-brick building were second-story porches where moms sat, keeping a watchful eye on a group of kids jumping rope and shooting hoops in their makeshift playground, the parking lot, below. A few potted plants lined random porches, most of which were withered from the ravages of a recent heat wave that plagued North Carolina. Drought season was in full swing, as the thirsty strip of brown grass that separated the complex from the road testified as it pleaded for rain.

I had parked my car along the street to avoid a basketball denting my hood and proceeded to look for Gene's apartment number emblazoned in bronze on his door: 4A. It was easy enough to find on the first floor, four doors in. A long minute after I knocked, the burgundy door creaked open, and I stumbled back when a burly mammoth of a man answered.

"Who are you, and what d'ya want?" he grumbled through a crack just big enough to show his six-foot-four frame. His white beard rested on his barrel chest, and his left hand disappeared behind his back. I wondered if a gun was in that hand and I considered running.

But instead I mustered my courage and stood my ground.

"Are you Gene Sanders?" I asked meekly, hoping it wasn't. This was not a man I wanted to interrogate.

"Who's askin'?"

"I'm Derek Worthington's nephew, Landon. I wanted to talk to you."

He humphed, then opened the door wider and waved me in. I took a hesitant step inside. Before closing the door, he peered out into the hallway. "You bring company?" he asked.

"No, sir."

As he shut the door, sure enough, he was holding a gun—a revolver. One that took a .38 Special cartridge.

"So you Danny's boy, eh?" he said, gesturing me toward a worn leather sectional in the living room. For a bachelor pad, it was immaculate. Not at all what I would expect from this Paul Bunyan lookalike.

The hardwood floors in the entry were polished to a shine, and I could see vacuum lines on the beige living room carpet. A cherry wood and glass coffee table sat in the center of the room, and a 50-inch TV hung from the far wall as SportsCenter highlights played in the background. The cream walls were bare but clean. And was that the smell of fresh-baked chocolate chip cookies coming from the kitchen?

Gene plopped onto the sofa and set the gun on a matching end table. "How's my man Derek? Ain't heard from 'im in a while."

"He's doing good," I lied. I had no idea how he was. I avoided him like the flu. "Though he's not what I'm here about."

"That so? Spit it out, boy."

As this gun-toting criminal with a face like forty miles of bad road eyed me skeptically, I almost decided to forget the whole thing. Almost. But Mia's challenge to step up for justice nudged at me, and damn the consequences. Besides, his home was too clean for him to spatter my blood all over the spotless carpet, so I figured I'd be safe from getting shot for nosing around his turf.

"Do you know why my dad's in jail?" I began, tossing my baited line into the water.

"Uh, yeaaaah," he said, stretching the word out. "Cuz of that there mansion robbery, right?"

I nodded. "I was wondering if you knew anything about it. I believe my dad's innocent, but I need to prove it. I hoped you could help me." I figured honesty from the get-go was the best tactic with someone who could pummel me with his pinkie.

"I don't know nothing 'bout it."

I had anticipated this reply. "My dad says you do. You, him, and Uncle Derek had planned the robbery together."

Clearly that was the wrong thing to say.

"You accusin' me of lyin'?" he seethed, resting his hand on his gun grip.

"No, sir. I'm just asking for the truth. I want to help my dad." I hoped my voice didn't sound as shaky as I felt.

"Look, I respect you lookin' out for family, so I'll be honest with ya. Originally the plan was that we'd do it together. But at the last minute your dad called it off, and I ain't had nothin' to do with it after that. Maybe he went back, maybe he didn't. I dunno. Alls I know is I wasn't involved after that, and I been clean ever since."

And yet the man's wariness and weapon screamed anything but the honest life. There had to be some kind of clue I could dig up to uncover the truth.

"Thank you for your time," I said, rising to my feet feeling hopeless. I wasn't cut out for this, no matter how much Mia encouraged me.

"Hope you find your guy," Gene said, walking me to the door.

Then a thought raced through my mind...almost too quickly to catch. I remembered an obscure detail in the police report. It was worth the risk of getting caught in a lie. "Oh, before I forget. Uncle Derek asked if I could get your number for him. He lost his cell phone and all his contacts."

"Sure. It figures—that knucklehead was always careless." He grabbed a pen and paper and jotted the number down before sending me on my way.

As I ambled to my car, my heart sank. Gene Sanders— aka Grizzle—was innocent...of the robbery, at least. But whatever other secrets he hid—secrets I had no intention of unearthing—were bad enough to compel him to answer the door holding a gun.

Chapter 9

2014

I just don't want to do it anymore," I whined like a four-year-old to Mia over lunch at one of our favorite Greek/Italian restaurants, Meelos. The atmosphere was simple comfort, the long-suffering staff tolerated my unusual order requests, and the food was authentically delicious—everything I preferred in a place to dine.

It had been a mentally exhausting day facing Gene, and I was ready to throw in the towel, especially after watching him write down his number with his left hand. Our robber was right-handed, according to the police report, so I had nothing. But Mia—never one to give up—perpetually pushed me onward with her gentle, sweet spirit:

"Landon, grow a pair."

My "lack of a pair" had been up for debate throughout the entire meal of fresh bread and homemade stuffed ravioli as I tried explaining to her that overturning a twenty-two-year-old conviction against my father was easier said than done. Indisputable proof—that's what I needed and didn't have. And considering my father had long ago been sentenced without an appeal, the cops weren't going to waste their resources helping me. Not while a killer—my sister's killer—was still on the loose, with new victims appearing every time I read the paper, so it seemed.

"If you believe your dad," Mia continued, "you need to keep looking for answers until you find them. I know it's not easy. Nice things come easy, but *great* things... those require sacrifice."

I groaned my accord, reluctant to cave, but I didn't feel like listening to more of Mia's pep talk. "Fine, you're right. I'll keep digging. I just don't know where to continue."

Mia pursed her lips in contemplation, mentally reviewing all I'd told her. "So your dad says only him, your Uncle Derek, and that Grizzle guy were involved. But obviously there was someone else—the person who told your Uncle Derek about the house in the first place. Who was that?"

"No clue. My dad doesn't know, and Uncle Derek wouldn't tell him."

"How about the old lady victim—Ruby Parker? Can you talk to her? And the witness listed on the police report—what about him? Those could be two leads. Maybe they know something that didn't come out in the original investigation."

She could be onto something. Ruby may have recalled details that didn't make it into the report—something unnoticed but important. It was worth a shot. Evan had printed a copy of the report for me, which included the key figures' full names and addresses. Typing the address into my cell phone, I mapped the drive. Only fifteen minutes from here.

"I'm gonna take a drive to visit Ruby, see if she still lives at the same address. Wanna tag along?"

Mia checked the time. "I wish I could, but I have to catch up on work tonight. Call me if you need inspiration... or a kick in the pants." Her playful grin evoked one of my own, and we hugged before she left.

Little did I know that it would be our last hug good-bye.

Twenty minutes later I stood at the front door of the address listed for Ruby Parker—the same home that was robbed twenty-two years ago, bringing my father's life to a grinding halt. It was a gorgeous stone and stucco house, two stories supported by impressive pillars... clearly worth more than I'd earn in a lifetime. Judging from the mini mansions lining the street, it had clearly remained an affluent neighborhood over the past two decades.

I rang the doorbell, which chimed to Beethoven's "Symphony No. 5" in a kaleidoscope of sound. Even the doorbell was pretentious.

An attractive thirty-something woman answered by the end of the first ring—which was a solid minute long.

"Can I help you?" she said brusquely, sweeping blond curls behind her shoulder.

"I'm looking for Ruby Parker."

"She's... no longer with us. Passed away a few years ago. I'm her niece. And who are you?"

I hadn't prepared to answer questions, so I went with what came naturally... and honestly. No point trying to be cloak-and-dagger about my intent.

"I'm so sorry for your loss," I said, unsure how emotionally fresh the loss was for the woman. "My name's Landon Worthington. My father was the one arrested for robbing her house a little over twenty years ago."

"Uh-huh." A curt nod accompanied her clipped reply.

"Some recent developments revealed that he might not be the one who did it, so I'm just trying to find out who may have."

The woman chuckled and muttered a barely audible "good luck with that" under her breath.

"I had hoped to ask Ruby some questions about that night, but it seems I'm too late."

"Sorry I can't help you. And quite frankly, I don't know if Aunt Ruby could've helped much anyways. She was going a little... senile in her old age. But just so you know, *technically* your dad—or whoever it was—didn't rob the place. Nothing was missing, from what I heard. The idiot knocked over a vase—an original fifteenth-century Ming Dynasty vase, mind you—when he was bumbling around in the dark. That's the only reason Aunt Ruby woke up in the first place—to find a million-dollar vase shattered to pieces. Any smart burglar would have been a little more careful. Regardless, nothing was stolen."

"Huh," I mumbled, dumbfounded. Now, my dad wouldn't know a priceless antique from an Ollie's Bargain Outlet special, but clumsily knocking it over? Not even if he was blitzed was he *that* ungainly. Despite his temper outbursts, he was generally a high-functioning drunk.

"And the guy who shot Aunt Ruby was a coward—no offense, her words," she continued. "Aunt Ruby got herself a gun after her husband, Uncle Howie, died because she felt unsafe by herself in this big old house. Uncle Howie collected shotguns and had taught her to shoot, so she had always felt comfortable with 'em. Got pretty good at it, and never went anywhere without her trusty pistol. She always joked about how she was a better shot than that joke of a burglar. As if he didn't even know how to hold or fire a gun."

"Really?" I asked. "What do you mean?"

"Oh, Aunt Ruby would tell the story at family gatherings of how the robber was fiddling with the safety when it went off—a total accident. And he was a klutz, tripping over things on his way out. Clearly a novice, and he actually apologized as he fled. She kind of felt bad for your dad all those years since she didn't think he could be a real criminal based on— her words again—his piss-poor burglary skills."

An interesting—and humiliating—take on my dad, to say the least. Though, while Dad hadn't owned a gun after I was born, he wasn't a novice with them. He practically grew up on the shooting range, and hunting was a prerequisite to be considered a man in his family. I doubted a few years would have stripped him of fundamental gun handling competence.

"Thanks, that actually helps a lot. The more I'm looking into this, the more I'm convinced it wasn't my dad. I'm just glad your aunt survived the shooting and lived to laugh about it."

"Oh yeah, we all got a chuckle. My aunt was a tough bird. God broke the mold with Aunt Ruby. Ask the neighbors— especially Bob. After her accident, he really stepped up to help take care of her, and basically did so up until her death. He probably knows more about her life than her own family does. Can't find neighbors like that anymore. Speaking of, you may want to ask him about that night. He was the only person who saw the getaway car, and probably the only neighbor who's still around here."

She pointed his house out, sweeping a finger toward the red brick manse next door. I thanked her before exchanging a lighthearted good-bye, doubting Bob would be of any more help than what the police report offered, but I figured it wouldn't hurt.

Five minutes later and about three hundred feet away, I stood face to face with a sixty-year-old version of Dwight Schrute from *The Office*. Friendly blue eyes peered out from behind 1980s-inspired silver wire-rimmed glasses, which lent him a bookish air. His greasy blond hair, shot through with streaks of gray, hung in his eyes, and he pushed it away as he greeted me warmly.

I introduced myself and my purpose for stopping by, and to my surprise, Robert Dillon—his friends and family called him Bob—invited me in.

"Thanks, Bob. A beautiful place you got here." My eyes couldn't help but widen with awe as I entered a marble-tiled entryway that led to a central staircase with a girth wide enough to fit three elephants side by side. Beyond the entrance was what appeared to be a living room I could play football in—if I had an athletic bone in my body, which I didn't.

"I feel like I was just 'Knockin' on Heaven's Door,'" I said with a forced laugh.

He stared at me, stone-faced, until my bad Bob *Dylan* pun finally registered with Bob *Dillon,* then he suffered a grin.

"Ah, I get it, you're having a little fun with my name. Lots of folks do," he said with a chuckle, then waved me to follow him to the living room.

"Have a seat," he offered.

I accepted, sinking into the cushions and suddenly ready for a nap. How could upholstery so fancy also be so comfortable? At first glance, I had imagined the contemporary style to be stiff and rigid—also what I assumed most rich people to be like—but so far I had been proven wrong twice in one visit. Shame colored my cheeks as Bob offered me a beer.

Ten minutes later we were chatting like two old college roomies, and when the mood felt comfortable, I segued into ancient history—the robbery he witnessed next door.

He sighed. "Boy, that was a long time ago. Never thought I'd be revisiting that night again. But I'm happy to tell you what I remember..."

Chapter 10

Ruby Parker had grown used to the low squeak of floorboards shifting at night. Even the thump in the living room downstairs could have been shrugged off as the *whoomph* of the heat pump kicking on this cold night. But the jarring sound of glass shattering—that was enough to wake Ruby from her usual shallow slumber as a news broadcast about a local Durham teacher droned on in the background of her bedroom.

She glanced at the television as a picture of Jeremy Mason popped up in the corner and the news reporter elaborated on the breaking news of charges being pressed against the science teacher for child molestation. Turning away from the television, she slipped out of bed, her ears attentive.

Ruby was a smart old gal, and she wasn't about to announce her presence to what she assumed had to be an intruder. After donning her robe, she reached for her Smith & Wesson .22 tucked under the edge of her mattress and wordlessly tiptoed to the bedroom door and listened. Somebody bumbling around. The squeal of a chair scraping along her hardwood floor. A low grunt.

It wasn't the stealthiest of intruders.

Pressing the gun to her thigh, she crept along the wall and decided to take a peek before shooting.

Her nimble steps descended the stairs, then padded around the landing toward the living room, which brought her face-to-backside with a masked intruder. Using his

49

gloved hand, he was bent over sweeping up shards of pottery from the floor—pieces of her very original and very valuable Ming vase.

Of all the things in her house to break, he stumbled into the priceless one...

Her sudden and emphatic "ahem" startled the mystery man, who bolted upright and pivoted around to face her in surprise. Tall and lean, he would have posed a fearsome threat, if only he didn't seem so awkward as he staggered backward.

In his right hand was a revolver, which she stared at with wide eyes. His gaze followed hers to his trembling hand, then slowly strayed to *her* much steadier hand where her own gun was firmly clenched... much more confidently than his own. With an apologetic "please don't shoot me," he fumbled with his piece, attempting to turn on the safety. Only, the fabric of his gloved fingers caught on the trigger, sending a shot into the room just as Ruby pivoted to shield her body with crossed arms.

A split second later, pain from the bullet's impact sent her to the floor, where she clutched the throbbing flesh of her shoulder. She stared incredulously at the ragged hole in her robe and nightgown, then at the neat, precise hole in her skin that was starting to bubble with blood.

"You ass!" she yelled. "You shot me!"

"Oh my God!" he yelped. "Are you okay?" He ran to her side, and seeing that the bullet only caught her in the shoulder, he scampered to the front door like a scared rabbit. "I'm so sorry!" he called behind him as the door swung open, a burst of cold air marking his disappearance into the darkness.

Ruby fought off her panic, willing herself to be calm.

"You're okay," she whispered, eyeing the flesh wound. "Just a little scratch."

Although the blood seeping down her arm warned that it was more serious than that.

A SECONDHAND LIE

She hoisted herself up and toward the open door, searching the street for a vehicle that might identify the intruder—a make, model, license plate number, anything at all. But there was no getaway car in sight, and the would-be burglar was long gone, apparently having escaped on foot.

Nursing her injury with a makeshift dishtowel tourniquet, she headed to the rotary phone and began to dial.

"What the hell just happened?" she murmured to herself as the line began to ring. She winced from the pain shooting across her shoulder. "And who was that masked man?" Ruby joked to herself, quoting the *Lone Ranger*, one of her deceased husband's all-time favorite TV shows.

Good ol' Ruby—always able to find the humor in any situation.

Chapter 11

Except that's not how Bob remembered it.

History often rewrites itself based on who is doing the telling.

Which doesn't make things simple when trying to dig beneath the fiction to find the facts.

"So you remember seeing my dad's vehicle pull away from the house after you heard the gunshot?" I clarified with a heavy sigh as Bob finished recounting his long-ago memory.

"That's right, I definitely saw a car haul ass outta there," Bob confirmed.

"Let me see if I've got this straight. You didn't see anybody flee on foot, just a car leaving the scene—a car with only one person inside, and no getaway driver?"

"Yup. That's about the size of it."

Skepticism squeezed my gut. I wondered how the assailant could flee the scene undetected after firing a gunshot in a ritzy neighborhood like this. According to the police report Evan had showed me, no other neighbors saw the car... or saw anything, for that matter.

My investigation was getting me nowhere closer to finding out who was behind it, or why. If it was indeed a random act, how did my dad's name get mixed in with it? All the missing links were only running me into more question marks.

"It just doesn't add up. My dad knew how to handle a gun, and he'd have been smart enough not to drive his own car, I'm sure. I just wish I could help him. He's innocent, and he's lost a daughter and so much of his life over something I don't think he did."

"Lost a daughter?" Bob asked.

"Yeah, my sister was murdered around the same time of this robbery. In fact, we're still trying to find her killer. I believe he may be responsible for other murders since then. It was a long time ago, but my dad was convicted of the robbery right after losing a daughter. I don't know how he's been able to survive what he's been through. I just want to help clear him so that he can get whatever's left of his life back before it's all wasted."

"I'm sorry to hear that. I kind of lost a child too. Not nearly the same thing, but the most painful experience I've ever endured, regardless."

"What happened?" I asked.

Bob shook his head, as if warding the buried memory away from pulling him into its grave. Silence reached up with skeletal fingers, clutching us both in a tense grip.

"Just a really bad divorce after I lost my job many years ago. My ex thought I was unfit to be a father so she took the kids and headed across the country, pretty much making it impossible for me to see them. Back then, in the early nineties, the mother always got full rights. She bad-mouthed me to everyone so much my kids didn't even want a relationship with me. It's been twenty years since I heard from them. I try to keep tabs on them online, but what I can find isn't much. I haven't even met any of my grandkids..." His words trailed off to a hoarse whisper of regret that couldn't capture the ache.

"I hear divorces can get ugly..." I said empathetically, knowing how broken my own parents' separation had left me and my sister.

"You have no idea. I almost lost my house and went bankrupt over it. Only reason I survived was because of Ruby's generosity. But my kids... I could never salvage a relationship with them no matter how much I tried." He lowered his head and fell silent.

"Is that why you helped Ruby so much after her injury?" I asked after a respectful moment.

53

Recalled from his hellish reverie, Bob's chin popped up defiantly. "What? Who told you that?" he asked guardedly.

The sudden shift in tone didn't escape my attention. He was clearly perturbed, but why? My suspicions piqued, I wanted to know more, but I'd need to probe deeper without scaring him off. "Ruby's niece said you were kind enough to help her recover after the shooting, and pretty much ever since. That was nice of you."

"Oh, yeah, I guess. It was the neighborly thing to do, right? I think maybe helping me with my debt was her way of thanking me after all the years."

Now, I wasn't one to scrutinize why people did what they did, but it seemed awfully coincidental to me that Bob, out of the kindness of his oversized heart, would suddenly assist an old lady for years on end with no reward except the collective admiration of the neighborhood. My sixth sense—and years of trust issues—told me there was more to Bob's story.

"Wow, years of service with no payment? I only wish I could claim such nobility. You should be knighted," I joked with a light chuckle, hoping to pull out more information.

"Nah, nothing noble. I just had a lot of free time… jobless and all that." With that, Bob slapped his thighs and rose from the couch, prompting me to do the same… without the answers I needed. "But clearly things worked out. I ended up starting my own company, and life ain't too bad," he continued with a shift toward the foyer.

"Thanks for all your time," I said, following him to the front door. "And I hope things with your kids work out. My dad never got that chance, but you never know what might happen. I'm clinging to that hope for my own family—that I free my dad and find my sister's killer. My family's been so destroyed, I need some kind of hope for justice, you know?"

"Don't we all want justice?" he asked. The hypothetical question lingered in the air as I thanked him again for his time and left, unsure where to go, what to do.

A minute later I sat in my car replaying the conversation, wondering what secrets Bob clung to. Then again, apparently everyone I knew harbored secrets these days—my mom, my dad... perhaps Uncle Derek?

With that thought tickling my mind, I pulled up my maps feature on my cell phone and typed in an address.

It was time to pay Uncle Derek a visit.

❧❦

Uncle Derek's ramshackle house was an eyesore from the outside—requisite derelict car up on cement blocks in a front yard whose knee-high grass desperately needed cutting, rotting love seat and La-Z-Boy chair decorating the cattywampus front porch—and an assault on all the senses once you entered. The foul reek of mildew and B.O.—and maybe even an unflushed toilet—made me catch my breath. The outdated olive carpet, a shaggy 1970s relic, was raggedy and stained with God knows what, and there were jagged spider-webbed cracks all over the plaster walls, where Derek had likely vented his rage in one of his booze- or meth-fueled binges. Roaches as tame as housecats, and almost as big, to my wondering eyes, made themselves at home among the heaps of beer cans and takeout containers. I was surprised the city hadn't condemned the place long ago.

"Hey, kiddo," Uncle Derek greeted me. "Can I git you somethin'—a beer? Coffee?"

"No thanks. I can't stay long, but I wanted to talk to you about something."

"Everything a'right?" he said, grabbing a can of Coors before falling into the sofa with a groan. He patted the filthy cushion next to him and said, "Take a load off, kiddo."

"No thanks, I'll stand." There was no point beating around the bush. "I wanted to know if you remember anything about the robbery my dad's doing time for."

He took a swig of beer, his eyes narrowing at me. "Why you askin'? That's ancient history, son."

"I don't think he did it, but I think someone close to him might have."

"You callin' me out on that there crime?" he asked, leaning forward and resting his elbows on his bony knees that wobbled under the weight.

By this point I was tired of the mental chess game. I knew the facts, and the facts pointed to the wiry, weaselly redneck sitting in front of me. "I know you owed money to some bad people. I also know the robbery was your idea. So please just tell me the truth, Uncle Derek. Did you let my dad take the fall for you?"

Uncle Derek's head bobbed slowly, as if assessing my motives. "Alls what you said is true. But your dad called it off, and..." he sighed heavily, then continued, "and I'm too chickenshit to pull off something like that by my lonesome."

It was the most sense Uncle Derek had ever spoken, and almost believable. That much was true—Uncle Derek was a coward. And the robbery was a solo endeavor. Even though it was an epic failure, I knew Uncle Derek. He'd never had the guts to take matters into his own hands... unless his life was endangered. Death was a pretty powerful motivator.

"How'd you pay off your lender if you had decided not to rob the place? Shouldn't you be dead by now?"

He laughed as if I'd told a joke, then said soberly, "Your mama. Gave me her grandma's engagement and wedding rings. Worth enough to pay off what I owed."

It figured my poor mother had been the one to get him off of Death's hook. The word *coward* was being generous.

Apparently Uncle Derek noticed the shame sweeping over my expression, because he felt the need to explain. "I never meant no harm, and I wasn't gonna ask your mama for help, but I didn't know where else to turn. They was gonna kill me, Landon."

With a wave I shushed him, my irritation swelling. "I know, I know. But that doesn't change the fact that *your* idea got my dad thrown in jail. You're his brother, and you dragged him into your mess, leaving my mom to clean it up for you. Maybe one of these days you'll man up and take responsibility for your actions."

56

A SECONDHAND LIE

"But I ain't done nothin' wrong!" he pleaded. "I swear."

I didn't know if Uncle Derek was innocent or not, but I wasn't going to get the truth no matter how hard I pushed. The man was a pathological liar.

"I can't take any more lies!" I yelled, giving vent to the storm of emotions swirling through me.

I never heard his defense as the screen door squealed shut behind me.

Chapter 12

A moment arrives when you helplessly watch the world crumble around you, and all you can do is limply watch. Once upon a time I would have mustered the courage to change things—with an iron fist, if needed—but any passion left had been tapped dry.

It wasn't so much that my investigation was going in circles. Or that my dad was in jail. Or that my sister's killer was still on the loose. Or that Mia was at arm's length. It wasn't any one of those single factors that led me down a path of desperation and despair. No, it was something inside myself that was deteriorating—my faith in humanity.

My faith in myself.

Once upon a time I trusted that all things happened for a reason. But that theory collapsed under the weight of pain. I'd lost so much, which was ironic because I had so little to begin with. All I could do was yield to the takers as they stole everything away from me—my sister, my father, my happiness... and I wondered if Mia would be next.

What decency still resided in my cold heart was ready to flee.

Heading nowhere in particular, I drove the minutes away, watching the homes and frolicking children pass by in a blur. Somehow the endless gray asphalt numbed me, leaving gaps of unaccounted-for time. When my brain eventually caught up with my location, I saw I was turning onto Ruby Parker's street. I pulled over in front of Ruby's house, wondering what had led me here.

A row of trees separated the two homes—Ruby and Bob's—and I started imagining the scene from twenty-two years ago unfolding. The eerie darkness of night. The gunshot. The robber fleeing from the house, parked where I currently sat, then peeling away. But why would he have parked here—in plain sight? Why not down the street to avoid his car being identified? Too many questions that led to illogical answers.

I didn't know what propelled me to get out of my car and briskly trot toward Bob's house. My hand involuntarily knocked, while my brain reminded me that I had already asked everything there was to ask. Well, maybe not everything...

He answered the door with a smile.

After apologizing for bothering him again, I wanted to know if he had any idea why the robber wouldn't have parked down the street.

"The details you're giving me don't make sense, Bob," I said, my statement proposing a challenge. "Why would the robber park out front? And how could he have driven away undetected—after firing a shot that woke the entire neighborhood—so quickly without a getaway driver?"

He shrugged off the flood of questions with a muted "I don't know," then shifted uncomfortably in the narrow sliver of doorway that separated us. The confrontation had clearly made him nervous as he avoided my steady glower. With a defensive stance, Bob crossed his arms over his chest, harboring within his closed heart a secret, a secret that I sensed could free my dad.

"You know, it was a long time ago," Bob explained, standing firmly between me and the expansive foyer behind him. "I honestly don't remember much about what happened, only that it was dark and I heard the gunshot and when I looked outside I saw a car speed away. Maybe the car I saw had nothing to do with the robbery—a coincidence. I feel bad that there's nothing else I can do to help."

Something about his wording nagged at me, but what, exactly? The chronology of events seemed to make sense... except... except for one thing. Could that be the clue I was searching for?

"You say you heard the gunshot and then the car sped away. About how much time took place between the gunfire and the car peeling away?"

"Hmm, I dunno. Maybe a minute or so. Why?"

And there it was. The red flag I'd been looking for, waving proudly.

I knew my dad's car, with its notoriously undependable nature, couldn't possibly have managed such a feat. No way could that car have been Dad's Ford Tempo without at least a ten-minute warm-up while someone pumped the accelerator.

Unless the car had been running the whole time the robber was in the house. Still, Bob's facts seemed riddled with holes.

But how could I possibly get Bob to trip over his error and tell me the truth? And what exactly *was* the truth? Was Bob covering for someone? Himself, perhaps? And if so, his word was the only evidence I had. The car was in some junkyard by now—the only thing that could prove my dad's innocence rusting into a pile of dust.

I had to pry deeper.

"Bob, are you sure about the timeline? I mean, my dad's car took on average ten minutes to start up, and that was on a good day. Are you sure you identified the right car?"

Scratching at the tip of his nose, Bob avoided my penetrating gaze and shifted his weight, his discomfort palpable now.

"Like I said, it was a long time ago and I don't remember much. I really gotta get going, though," he said with an uncomfortable chuckle.

Guilt. I read guilt between the lines, in the awkward stance, in the nervous energy. But clearly Bob wasn't going to give me anything without a fight. I had no idea how to force him to reveal his hand.

Then I considered another tactic.

"Well, thanks for your time, Bob. I really appreciate it. I have a friend on the police force who offered to run bullet ballistics to see what gun the bullet was fired from—a revolver that used a .38 Special caliber. They're pulling gun purchase records around the date of the robbery, so we'll have a name soon. Would you like for me to keep you posted when they discover something?" A bold lie, sure, but it was all I had up my sleeve. I knew the bullet and casing were long gone, but it was a bluff that I hoped Bob would fall for.

"Oh really?" he said shakily, as if wakened from a dream. "Yeah, yeah, keep me informed..." he added cagily. "I appreciate you stopping by, but I really need to go."

With that he swung the door shut so quickly that the pocket of air ruffled my hair.

But I wasn't done with Robert Dillon. I knew his next move, even if he didn't.

An hour later I sat watching Bob pull out of his driveway in a silver Mercedes-Benz C-Class. Giving myself half a dozen car lengths between us, I followed him to the local Kroger grocery store. Curiously, he pulled around the back of the store to where several Dumpsters lined a brick wall. The hair on the back of my neck bristled.

I watched as he got out, carrying a grocery bag, then I discreetly exited my car.

"Don't you get public garbage service?" I asked loudly across the vacant space.

Bob's body jerked in surprise at the sound of my voice.

"Are you following me?" he voiced angrily.

"Are you trying to discard evidence?" I retorted with sarcasm.

"I don't know what you're after, Landon, but you need to mind your own business before you get hurt."

"Make me." As the words came out I realized I sounded ten years old, and an image of Pee-wee Herman flitted through my mind.

"If you insist." The grocery bag caught the breeze and blew away as Bob pointed a revolver straight at me. Yet his confidence wavered with his quaking hand—a flashback to what Ruby must have witnessed.

"Bob, you're not a killer. You know what the right thing to do is," I said, hoping my soothing voice was talking his adrenaline down. With my hands up in surrender, I took several faltering steps forward, until I stood a mere few feet from the barrel. At this distance, even a wobbly shot would likely be lethal.

"You just had to dig it all back up, didn't you? And for what? No one got hurt!" he screamed.

A bead of sweat popped up on Bob's forehead. Then another. The man began sweating like he'd just stepped into a sauna. With a slanted look I watched him squirm under my scrutiny.

"No one got hurt?" I echoed angrily. "My father lost a lifetime because of that false conviction! I lost a dad for most of my life. My mom lost a husband. Dammit, man, I'd say that a *lot* of people got hurt. Not to mention, Ruby was shot. The only consolation out of all of this was that my sister died before having to watch her father go to jail. At least she was spared the embarrassment and pain. Someone should pay— the person who did it. You. They're going to find you. The bullet will point to exactly who fired the shot, and if you're not willing to come forward on your own, the punishment will be a lot worse."

My rant was derailing, and I couldn't heft my thoughts back on track as the words spilled from my diarrheic lips.

"I think this conversation is over," he cut in, leaping forward and pushing the muzzle against my forehead.

Despite the strong urge to crap my pants, I studied him, watching the perspiration drip down his upper lip.

"Don't make this worse. You kill me, you're guilty of murder. That's a life sentence. Now's your chance to do the right thing, Bob. Put the gun down and turn yourself in."

He stood stoically, silently, but I knew panic raged beneath the surface.

My logical appeal wouldn't budge him. But maybe, just maybe, an empathetic soul would.

"Please," I begged. "You know what it's like to lose everything that matters. Don't let an innocent man suffer any longer for something he didn't do."

I watched the consideration lighten Bob's eyes as they rested on mine, searching me for courage, a silent plea. He wanted to do the right thing and set the truth free, but the icy fingers of fear held him back.

A heavy sigh shook his thick chest. The hand clutching the gun trembled as his arm finally dropped.

"I can't lie anymore. I've lost all there is to lose. I'm the one who robbed Ruby. I'm the one who shot her."

Chapter 13

I'm sorry it took me this long to come clean," Robert Dillon finally mustered after his admission fell from his lips. "I didn't mean to hurt anyone, I swear."

It all made sense.

The divorce had left him broke. He was about to lose his house, his kids, his wife—everything. He needed money, and Lord knows Ruby had plenty to go around. Not to mention, it was an easy target—his elderly next-door neighbor. In, out, no one any the wiser.

Until he accidentally shot her. Which was why he so generously took care of her for all those years.

But a question nagged at me as Bob's apology spilled forth.

"Why my dad—why tell the cops it was his car you saw pull away?"

He laughed a shallow chuckle of grief and remorse.

"Gene Sanders—you know, your uncle's friend, the one everyone calls Grizzle—well, he worked as a security guard at the software development company I used to work at. Eventually he left, but we kept in touch... mostly for poker games. Originally I went to Gene with the idea of robbing Ruby 'cause of my financial woes. So he proposed the plan to your uncle, which was perfect since your uncle apparently was in some kind of financial trouble and all too eager to do it. Your dad was just a casualty. So, the plan was that your uncle and dad would rob Ruby, Gene and I would be the fence for the stolen goods, and we'd split whatever money we made. I figured it'd be enough to pay for the divorce attorney and catch up with my debt. But when your dad put a stop to the whole thing, I knew I was ruined."

64

A SECONDHAND LIE

He paused, rubbed his temple, then palmed the back of his neck, his fingers massaging the knotted muscles. "You have no idea the stress I was under."

With a roll of his neck I heard the faint crack of bones. "Stress, guilt, whatever it is has been plaguing me ever since. Anyways, I figured I'd just do it on my own. Bought a gun—not to shoot her, but just so that I looked like a legit robber. Playing the part, you know? Didn't even realize I had left bullets in it from when I bought it."

I nodded understanding, still baffled by the extreme measures one would go through just to keep up appearances.

"So I winged it. Didn't expect Ruby to catch me in the middle of it. Shooting her was an accident—I freaked. When I fled, I knew the cops would ask questions and I wanted them off my scent, so I said it was your dad's car that was there. Gene had already told me what he drove so I knew what to say if they ever showed up at my door."

"Did you also call in the anonymous tip?"

"I don't know anything about that."

"So you figured you'd pin it on an innocent man—and you still sleep at night?"

"To be honest, I was pissed at your dad for ruining the plans in the first place. It was too easy, and I figured he probably deserved jail anyways since Gene painted him as the criminal type. I never knew the guy, or anything about your sister's murder, I swear. I guess he was just in a bad place like I was. I feel rotten about everything now."

It took a minute or two to let the explanation sink in. Despite the sorrow lingering between the lines of his words and his strained brow, the confession soured any sense of compassion I had for him an hour ago. In my opinion, he deserved to lose everything.

"So you lied to the police about it—gave false testimony to cover your own butt?" I clarified, already knowing the answer.

His head bobbed affirmation, his eyes shamefully cast downward. "I looked at it as a little white lie, you know? Just stretching the truth. Now I realize it was a lot more than that."

One little lie destroyed an entire family.

But the most important question hadn't been asked, hadn't been answered.

"Will you step forward and tell the cops what you've told me?"

It was a long interlude before he replied. So long I wasn't sure if he'd ever answer. Eventually he did... cautiously.

"Yes, I'll come clean. Your dad will go free."

For the first time in my thirty-eight years I felt a surge of hope. A surge of freedom from the lies that held my family hostage—the mysteries that we could never solve, the ache that we could never soothe, the secrets that imprisoned us. My father would finally be free. One step toward healing my broken family. One step toward giving Alexis what she had always yearned for as a kid: wholeness.

If unqualified me could figure out who took away my father's freedom, maybe I could find Alexis's killer after all.

Chapter 14

I left feeling like the straightjacket that had bound my emotions for decades was at last unfastened. Justice tasted sweet today. My dad would be exonerated, adding one more step toward closure to all the loose ends that encumbered my life.

Yet there was one tiny detail that nagged at me:

Who had left the anonymous tip that it was my dad at the crime scene?

Who entombed his fate?

I'd probably never find out, but it irked me that some mystery person was out to get my dad... but why?

I headed home to tell my mom the good news, shrugging off the looming questions. Did it really matter? Perhaps some answers were best unknown and left in the past, as long as that's where they stayed.

When I walked into my living room, I found my mom sitting on the sofa sipping tea and reading a book. A floral scent wafted up from her mug, an inviting and calming aroma. She looked up and smiled.

"Hey there," she greeted me.

"Got some great news, Mom," I said, cutting to the chase. The news was too good to play around with pretext.

"What's that, honey?" she said, inviting me to sit as she patted the cushion next to her and placed the book on the coffee table.

"Dad's gonna be a free man." I waited a beat for her brain to catch up.

"What? What are you talking about?" Her face scrunched up with perplexity.

"I found out who committed the robbery that put Dad behind bars, and he's agreed to step forward. Apparently it was the next-door neighbor."

Uncertainty engulfed her as the weight of my news sank in, then finally understanding slipped past her confusion. Her jaw dropped and her eyes widened. "Really? Are you serious?"

"As a heart attack."

"So... your dad's going to be released from jail?" Her wrinkled hands clutched mine with a grip I didn't know she had in her.

I nodded, noting the wide grin spreading across her face, lifting her cheeks that were now flushing with excitement. Apparently it was better news than I thought.

A moment later her arms flung around me, pulling me into a hug as a squeal escaped her lips. "Oh, honey, thank you. Thank you!"

As she babbled her thanks between joyous sobs, she pulled back and held me at arm's length, staring at me with admiration.

"Wow, Mom, I wasn't expecting quite this level of... excitement. I didn't realize you missed him this much."

"It's more than that, honey. So much more..." She swiped at a cascade of tears along her cheekbone, then blinked back another rush of them.

"What do you mean?" I asked, afraid to know what she was referring to.

Her eyes avoided mine, then darted to her hands, which she folded and unfolded in her lap now. "I don't know that I should tell you, Landon."

"Mom—no more lies. No more secrets. Please. I deserve the truth, don't you think?"

Gulping down a pocket of suffocating air, I waited for her explanation.

"Okay, I'll tell you. But please understand that this was your father's decision as well. Not just mine." She paused.

"Fine, just tell me," I urged, my patience wearing thin.

"The day the police showed up to question me about your father's involvement, I called in an anonymous tip saying it was him."

"What?" I yelled. "That was *you*? Why?"

"It's complicated," she blustered.

"Try me." My voice was stern, unshakable.

"I guess when the police talked to the neighbor and got his eyewitness account, he said he saw your father's car at the robbery. When the cops came around asking me about it, I knew your dad was innocent. Like I said, he'd been here—in front of our house—the whole time. But your dad was concerned your Uncle Derek was involved in the robbery somehow, and that if your dad didn't do time for the robbery then your Uncle Derek would. Your dad was trying to protect his little brother—you know how it's ingrained in him. So your dad asked that I call in a tip saying it was him so that the cops wouldn't eventually find their way to your uncle's doorstep. I mean, we didn't know what type of people Derek was doing business with and just how much trouble he could get into if the cops started looking into his... *activities*."

She took a breath, then continued, "I guess our plan worked in a way since your uncle's managed to stay mostly clean ever since, hopefully not getting involved again with those *lenders*, or whatever they're called—"

"Loan sharks," I interjected, realizing just how naïve she really was.

"Yeah, them, but we didn't expect your dad's punishment to be so severe. We thought he'd get a year, tops. Our attorney—who wasn't worth a damn—told us the judge was probably trying to set an example by using your father, since his term was up. I was shocked at the sentencing he got, but by then it was too late and we couldn't afford to appeal it."

Apparently they had thought the decision through. But there was one thing my parents didn't consider. One monumental thing.

"How do you know the loan sharks aren't responsible for Alexis's murder?" I asked.

"I've often wondered that," she replied with a weighted sigh, "but if indeed they did it, for what purpose? It's not like killing my baby girl was going to get them their money. Unless it was to make a point. But I got Derek the money to pay them off, so why hurt us after the fact?"

"Yeah, I know you sold your grandma's rings."

Mom shrugged, and her eyes dampened. "I don't have a daughter to pass them down to anymore. Why hold on to them?"

"Are you sure he used the money to clear the debt, though?"

"I can't go down that road thinking that way—that your uncle is somehow responsible for Alexis's murder. Otherwise your father sacrificed his life for his brother only to lose everything. No... I can't accept that."

She vehemently shook her head, closing her eyes against any possibility that the loan sharks were connected to my sister's murder.

"Your father accepted the blame to save his brother, to make amends for his failures, and to give us the freedom to heal without his bad influence. I'm healed. And he's healed. He used the time to get sober. And now he'll be free and we can start over, mending our lives together. Good came from it. I can't strip that away, not now after having lost so much."

Her heartfelt explanation pained me, like stitches mending a gaping wound. All I could do was accept it and exchange my lingering ache from the lies for the anesthesia of faith.

The depths of my soul opened, and I understood completely now. I realized why she had waited for him all these years, why they never fought the charges, why Dad never reached out to me from jail. All the whys joined together in a beautifully tangled web, revealing the purpose of his sacrifice and the reason for the lies. He needed to step away *from* us *for* us—his love was that profound, although buried under a jagged exterior of selfish indulgence. Now those chains were unbound and he could be who he always wanted to be, with his weaknesses finally laid to rest.

That's when I knew that one day all of my own anguish would also rest in peace.

Chapter 15

Jennifer Worthington picked up today's *News and Observer*, seething as she waved the front-page article in the air:

DURHAM MIDDLE SCHOOL TEACHER CONVICTED OF MOLESTING STUDENT

A Durham teacher was convicted Tuesday of taking indecent liberties with a minor after inappropriately touching one of his students. The scandal made headlines when the story broke in February.

Jeremy Mason, a science teacher in the Durham public school system, pleaded not guilty, and although he will be registered as a sexual offender, he received what some in the community are calling a light sentence. He had been teaching at the school for two years and is now on indefinite administrative leave.

Mason was accused of luring a minor female student, whose name the News and Observer is withholding, into his sixth-grade science classroom to discuss her test results, then making inappropriate advances toward the girl, which the victim's mother quoted included "fondling and touching." When Principal Rodney Williams was questioned about the details, he stated that the victim claimed she "was threatened with a failing grade if she didn't comply."

Durham police conducted an investigation that eventually led to Mason's arrest and conviction in a Durham district court. Due to insufficient physical evidence and written testimony from a fellow minor student who claimed to have overheard the victim boasting about her plans to frame Mason, the judge sentenced Mason to a three-year probation, the minimum sentence for a sexual offense.

"Children are notoriously unreliable witnesses, and we can't always know what the raw truth is," Principal Williams commented. "There's a big gray area in between the lines when it comes to what middle-schoolers say. While we don't know if Mr. Mason actually committed the crime, we can't allow further scandal to distract kids from learning. It was with a heavy heart that I was forced to place him on administrative leave."

Mason, a lifelong Durham resident, has received numerous death threats since the allegations surfaced, according to police. Citizens angered by the verdict protested briefly outside the courthouse. At press time Mason could not be reached for comment.

Sitting across from Jennifer on a recently purchased Goodwill sofa, clutching a mug of lukewarm coffee in both hands, was the man of the hour: Jeremy Mason. Now a pariah, and all because of one hateful and vindictive girl's lies.

Jennifer caressed the burnt orange corduroy of the matching chair catty-corner him, reluctant to adjust to the latest living room furniture additions. For some reason everything felt too final, removing the chair Alexis had been murdered in. As if keeping the recliner would have kept Alexis alive. But the girl's blood had soaked into the fabric too deep to clean, and the image of her near-dead body sprawled out across the arm of the chair was etched too intimately on her soul. A single piece of furniture had been a millstone around Jennifer Worthington's neck—a constant reminder of death and pain and anguish. She had no choice but to toss it, burying it in some dump along with the memories of her daughter.

At least for now that's where the memories would remain.

Maybe someday remembering wouldn't be so hard.

Today was the first time she'd been distracted from the grief since losing her daughter. Jeremy Mason's trial and conviction revived what was left of her emotions—a touch of empathy for his own loss of life.

"Don't worry, Jeremy. Things will smooth over from what that Renee Clark girl said. Even the judge didn't buy it." Unfortunately, Jennifer's feeble attempt at consoling Jeremy after his trial the day before proved fruitless, as she had expected. People didn't bounce back from things like this overnight... if ever.

His lips drooped into a broken frown, as if a sob sat on the verge of his lips.

"I just don't know how to feel, Jen. I hate that brat. She set out to destroy me, and why? Because of a poor grade? I'm so angry, so pissed I could—" His fist pounded the stained coffee table, punctuating the anger boiling within him as a crumb-littered plate trembled. But he didn't dare finish the sentence. True, Renee Clark had been his albatross, ruining his life, but after Jennifer's recent loss of her daughter, he chose his words carefully. Jennifer's wound was too fresh.

Jeremy glanced into Jennifer's eyes, saw the compassion and pity there, and looked away. "Don't mind me," he muttered. "I'm just at a loss for what to do. I want Renee to pay for what she's done, but what can I do? It's a frustrating position to be in, and I feel so helpless."

Jen rested a hand on his shoulder and squeezed tenderly. "We'll figure it out." Under his tense shrug, Jen's hand dropped away.

"How? I'm a registered sex offender now. I'll never be able to teach. I'm jobless. I'll be homeless soon too, since God knows no one will hire me to even flip burgers. You tell me, Jen, what's to figure out. My well of hope has run dry. All because of that spoiled little brat and her big mouth."

An awkward moment passed. His words spoke of the harsh reality of lies, yet Renee was just a young girl who was too naïve to realize the power she held and the fate she could pass on to another.

"I know you're upset, Jeremy, but she's a kid. A stupid, reckless one, yes, but still a kid."

Jeremy jumped up from his seat, clearly too angry to listen to any defense of the spiteful monster that had turned his life inside out.

"Look, I appreciate you being here for me, but you've got your own worries to deal with."

Yet voicing those worries... few people had mustered the courage to speak the words of sympathy out loud. It had only been two weeks since Alexis's murder, with no leads on who had done it, no justice or healing in sight. It was the elephant in the room that people tiptoed around, afraid of the wreckage that recognizing it aloud would cause.

The hush grew thick. Then Jennifer straightened her back and lifted her chin.

"I can't bring Alexis back from death. But maybe I can help you get your life back together."

He nodded solemnly, the sadness looming around them as Tragedy raped them until they were empty shells walking numbly through life. First, the loss of Jennifer's only daughter, her only chance at a better future. A future with grandbabies and mother-daughter pedicures and girl gossip over tea. Things she had never done before but suddenly needed to do now.

Then there was Jeremy's career and reputation and passion burned at the stake. All hopes and dreams felt misplaced that day, lost in a gust of wind that took them too swiftly.

"I never knew it was her who tried to help me..." Jeremy spoke softly.

"Who—Alexis?" Jennifer asked.

"Yeah, I wish I would have known she was the girl who spoke up on my behalf."

"Why do you say that?" Jennifer probed, uncertain of what he was trying to say.

"Just that if I had known she came to you with what she heard in the bathroom, maybe things would be different. Maybe I could have saved her too."

"How, Jeremy? How could you have saved her?" Jennifer spat, her voice skewering his statement. "I should have been here, but I wasn't. And now she's dead."

"I'm sorry," he whispered softly. "I just wish I could have known what she did for me before she was—"

Brutally murdered. Viciously killed. Those were the words he couldn't finish, but Jennifer knew them by heart.

"You want to thank my baby girl? Find her killer. That's how you can thank her," Jennifer replied curtly.

Little did Jennifer know of Jeremy's role in the saga of what happened to twelve-year-old Alexis Worthington, for she was too far trapped in her own emotional cage to see what swirled around her. Answers lurked in the shadows, and true identities hid behind masks. One day all would be revealed. The sun would shepherd in another revelation on another day—just not today.

A SECONDHAND LIE

In fact, the sun wouldn't shine for another twenty-two years.

Twenty-two years later their lives would clash in an epic tale as Alexis's killer would finally emerge. But this isn't that story. This is the story of resurrecting hope where there once was none. An account of justice. A tale of new beginnings when you thought you'd run out.

Second chances aren't fiction. As Jeremy and Jennifer and Landon and Dan discovered through the aches of life, lies eventually surface, bringing in the nurturing healing of truth.

Epilogue

2014

Dear Landon:

I write to you from Durham County Detention Facility after my confession for my part in the robbery. According to my lawyer, I'll be in and out in no time with barely a slap on the wrist since I 'fessed up on my own. Under normal circumstances one would think I'd be ticked off at you for unraveling my past sins, but not today. Instead, a thank you for the push up to the ledge is in order.

Why?

Because my life is finally whole again.

For the first time in twenty years I saw my daughter. I don't know how she caught wind of what happened, but she showed up out of the blue to visit me in jail... bringing along the most beautiful baby girl I've ever seen—my granddaughter Isabel. We spent the hour catching up and me apologizing for not being able to keep her in my life all these years. But more than that, she's actually living in Raleigh now and wants to rekindle our relationship. She even offered to mediate between me and her brother, but all in due time.

It's amazing how something I thought would ruin me ended up saving me. I finally got the guilt off my chest, my *daughter back, and for the first time in decades I'm happy. Ironic that jail would make me whole.*

Thanks, Landon, for prodding me to do the hard but right thing. At least your father will be out soon so that you can be reconciled. He should be proud of the son he raised.

I hope they find your sister's killer and that you find peace. I know what it's like to feel turbulence in your heart every day, so if that moment to grab serenity comes, take it. You may only get one chance. Don't leave it "Blowin' in the Wind." Another bad Bob Dylan joke. Now we're even, my friend.

Your Friend,
Bob Dillon

The stars dotting the inky sky tugged at my heart while I re-read the last paragraph a second time from my back porch. The metal chair creaked under me as I shifted to gaze up at the black expanse. The mantle of responsibility for my sister's death weighed heavily upon my shoulders tonight, blanketing my life with the taint of regret.

A pang of sorrow eclipsed my momentary optimism as I read Bob's message. While I was mere weeks away from reuniting with my father once the acquittal process was over, it wouldn't bring back Alexis from the dead. Only justice against her killer could part the clouds that darkened my world.

As I folded the letter back up and slid it into the envelope, I wondered if Mia was that "moment to grab serenity" that Bob referred to. My feelings for her were a 10,000-piece puzzle that moment by moment came together, a kaleidoscope of random colors creating a harmonic image that captured something more beautiful than I ever imagined.

I couldn't put a tag on it—love, friendship, family, whatnot. She was more than that to me.

While Mia sacrificed everything to rescue my sister's memory, she was in fact tossing a life preserver into my turbulent life as well. Was she even aware of how much she meant to me, that she had become my compass through the brine of life? I doubted it. Mia Germaine was a precious and courageous soul, one that I cherished more than my own life.

When she vowed to find my sister's killer, I knew she wouldn't give up until the job was done, even if the task took her own life. What better friend was there than that? My despair buckled under her love.

Together we would put an end to a serial killer's growing list of victims. We were only one step behind him—and his latest victim, Lilly Sanderson, would be his last. The Triangle Terror's reign would soon be over.

Closing my eyes, I conjured a picture of her face—those vibrant and passionate hazel eyes, her chestnut hair that tickled her shoulders when it swayed back and forth in a ponytail, her deeply intelligent mind. So beautiful inside and out.

I didn't deserve her.

But I needed her.

I wondered if she needed me too.

Not in the way the world would assume. I didn't want to make her my wife or possess her. I simply wanted her to know the truth about how I felt, who I was—to bare my soul to her. And maybe catch a glimpse of hers too.

At that moment I made a decision, one of the hardest I ever faced. I would profess the truths hidden in my soul to Mia ... and damn the consequences. Even if it cost me everything.

I was prepared to lose it all, and I welcomed it. Mia was worth it.

As I allowed a hazy calm to envelop me, I pictured how the scene would play out. It wouldn't be pretty; it wouldn't be perfect. But it would be ours.

Continue The Killer Thriller Series with *A Secondhand Life.*

If you've enjoyed *A Secondhand Lie,* I'd be honored if you'd share that by reviewing the book. If you're kind enough to write a review, email me at pamela@pamelacrane.com and I'll thank you personally with a free gift!

Feel free to browse my other titles at www.pamelacrane.com. Find an error in one of my books? I'd love to fix it, since even the best editors miss things (they're only human). Please email me at pamela@pamelacrane.com.

If you'd like to be notified of my upcoming releases or enter my giveaways, join my mailing list at www.pamelacrane.com for chances to win free prizes and pre-release offers.

Author's Note

This is only the beginning. Landon Worthington's path toward redeeming his family and avenging his dead sister has only begun in this companion story to the full novel, *A Secondhand Life.*

Who murdered Alexis two decades ago, and why? And is the serial killer the "Triangle Terror" the same killer behind her death?

Does Landon ever get the chance to confess his secrets to Mia Germaine?

These questions and more are revealed in the sequel that critics call:

"A spellbinding and intense tale with a refreshingly innovative premise…"

"A mind-bending, intelligent thriller that will pull you in until you're breathless with intrigue…"

Thank you for sharing Landon's journey with him as he uncovers the top layers of lies that have buried his family. I hope you will embark on finding his sister's killer in the next installment, *A Secondhand Life.*

Want more from Pamela Crane?

Pretty Ugly Lies

What causes a woman to murder her whole family?

Jo's idyllic life would make most people jealous. Until one day her daughter is abducted and the only way to find her is to unravel her dark past.

Ellie is a devoted wife... until she discovers the pain of betrayal. Now vengeance is all she can think about.

Party-girl Shayla knows how to hide her demons. But when she's confronted with a life-shattering choice, it will cost her everything.

June knows suffering intimately, though the smile she wears keeps it hidden.

Soon the lives of these four women intersect and one of them is about to snap...

From USA TODAY best-selling author Pamela Crane comes "a thought-provoking domestic noir novel perfect for fans of Liane Moriarty and B.A. Paris ... A chilling look at the secrets mothers will hide for the sake of their families, and the gruesome reality of what can break an everyday woman."

Four lives. Four lies. One killer among them.

What lies are *you* hiding?

Little Deadly Secrets

The deadliest secrets lie closest to home...

From *USA Today* bestselling author Pamela Crane comes an addictively readable domestic suspense novel about friendship, motherhood ... and murder.

Three best friends. Two unforgiveable sins. One dead body.

Mackenzie, Robin, and Lily have been inseparable forever, sharing life's ups and downs and growing even closer as the years have gone by. They know everything about each other. Or so they believe.

Nothing could come between these three best friends . . . Except for a betrayal.

Nothing could turn them against each other . . . Except for a terrible past mistake.

Nothing could tear them apart . . .
Except for murder.

PAMELA CRANE is a USA TODAY best-selling author and professional juggler. Not the type of juggler who can toss flaming torches in the air, but a juggler of four kids, a writing addiction, and a horse rescuer. She lives on the edge (her Arabian horse can tell you all about their wild adventures while trying to train him!) and she writes on the edge...where her sanity resides. Her thrillers unravel flawed women who aren't always pretty. In fact, her characters are rarely pretty, which makes them interesting...and perfect for doing crazy things worth writing about. When she's not cleaning horse stalls or changing diapers, she's psychoanalyzing others.

Discover more of Pamela Crane's
books at
www.pamelacrane.com

Printed in Great Britain
by Amazon

29041094R00054